AF268754

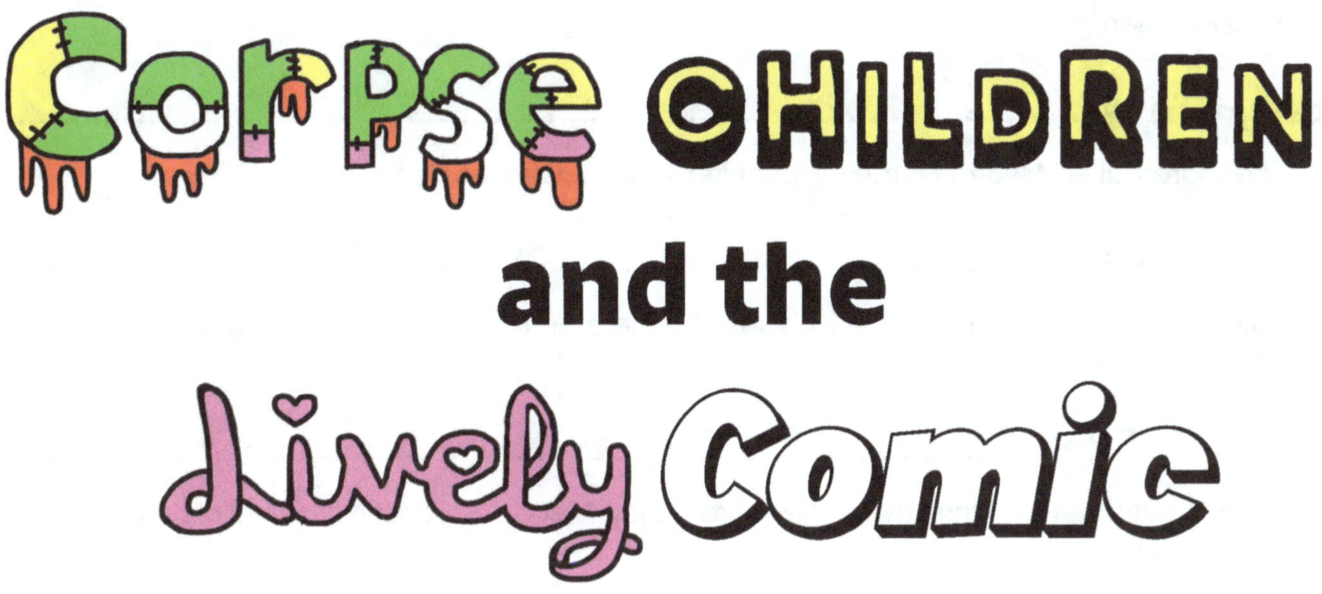

Corpse CHILDREN
and the
Lively Comic

Corpse Children and the Lively Comic

Edited by Rebecca Migdal

Design and cover art by:
Mason Higgins, Nicole Kolakowski,
Dempsey Langan, Jennifer Pagan
Ayden Pigeon and the
ESU Illustration Class of 2024

Corpse Children Logo: Nicole Kolakowski

TABLE OF CONTENTS

ACID DRAG EXPERIMENT

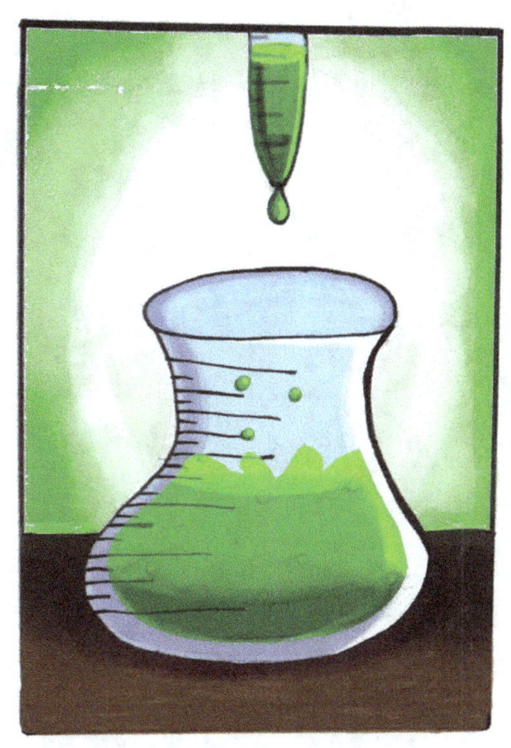

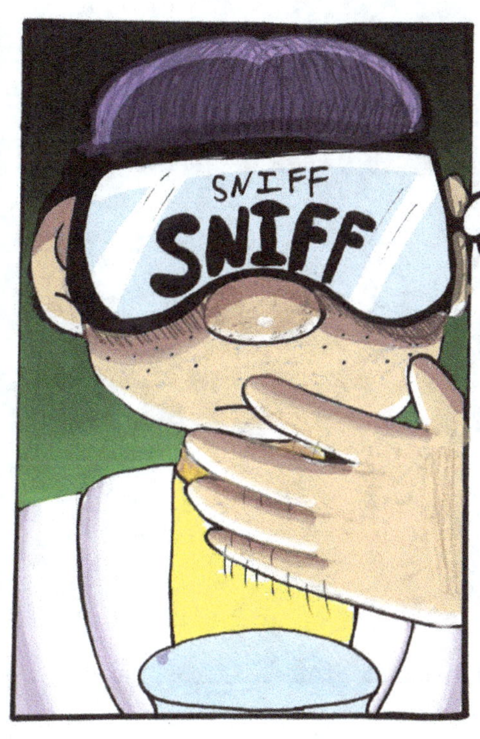

SNIFF
SNIFF

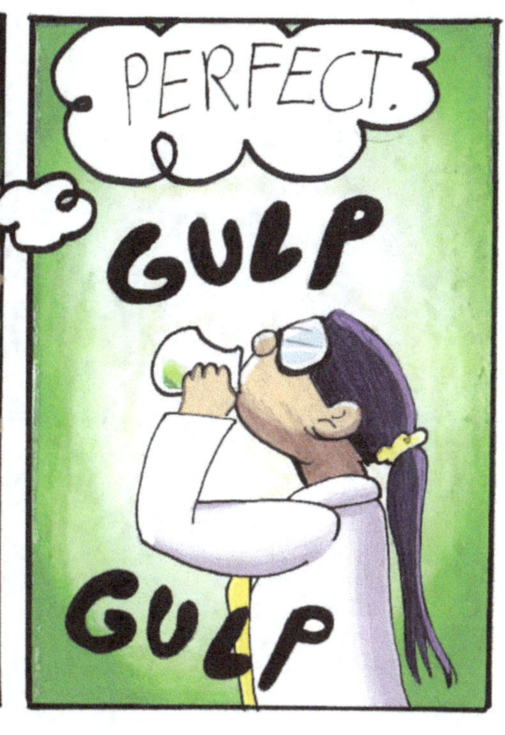

PERFECT.
GULP
GULP

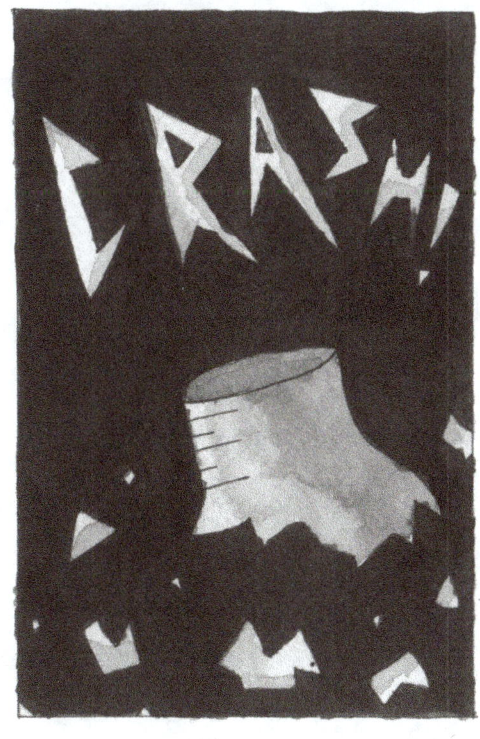

CRASH!

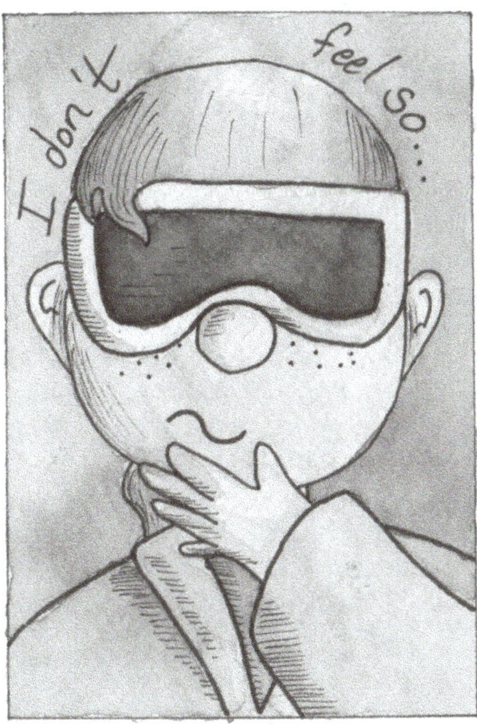

I don't feel so....

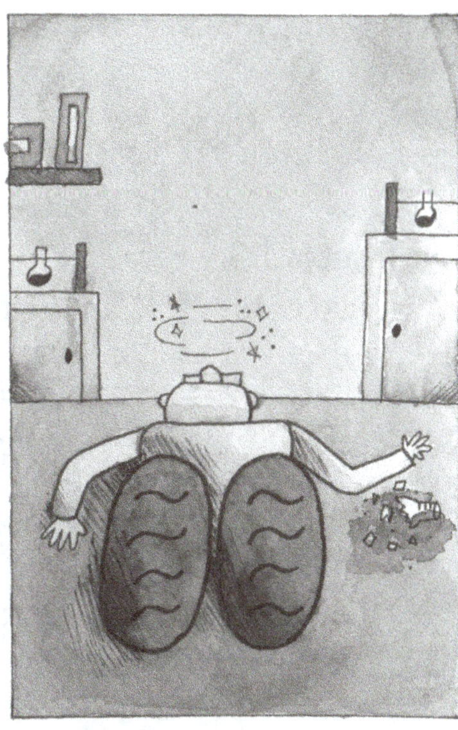

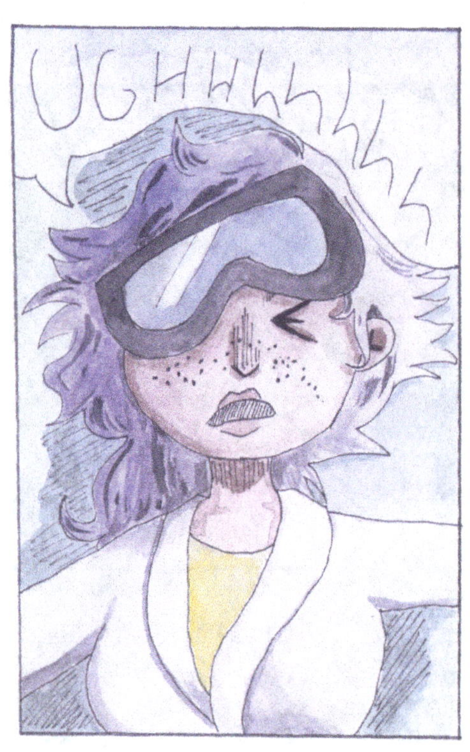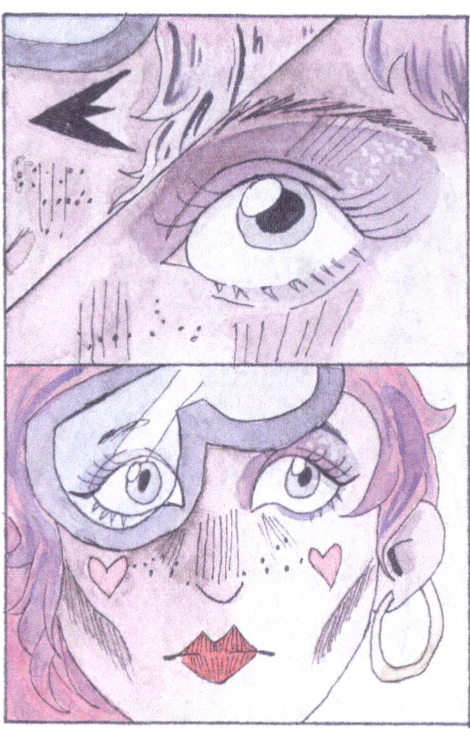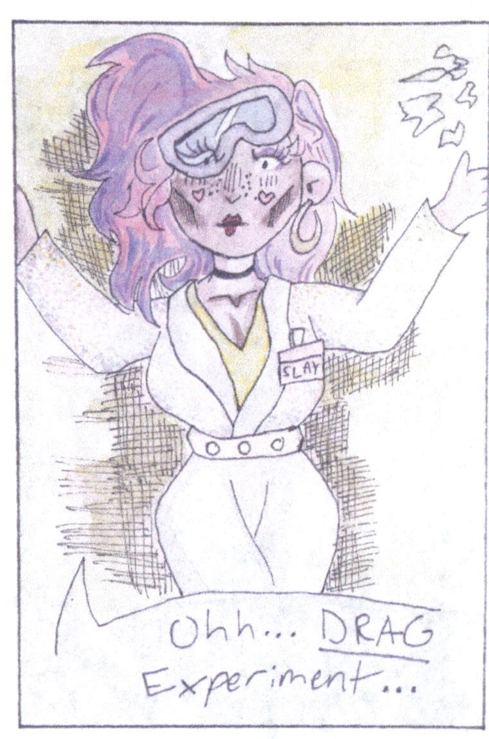

UGHHHHHH
Ohh... DRAG Experiment...
SLAY

ACiD DRAG EXPERiMENT

Panels 1-3
Illustrator, Ink, and Color: Spike Harris; Digital: Christopher Light

Panels 4-6
Illustrator, Ink, and Ink Wash: Emily Brier

Panels 7-9
Illustrator: Mia Jones; Ink: Kiersten Kozlowski; Water Color: Kalista Weed

ANARCHY BABY!

CASPER SAEZ

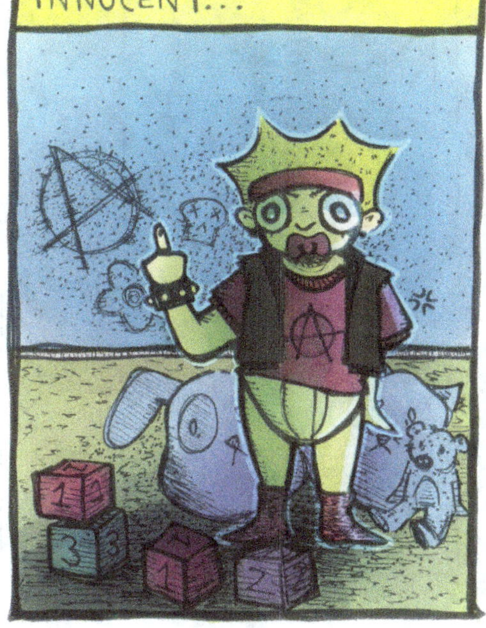

ANARCHY BABY MAY LOOK INNOCENT...

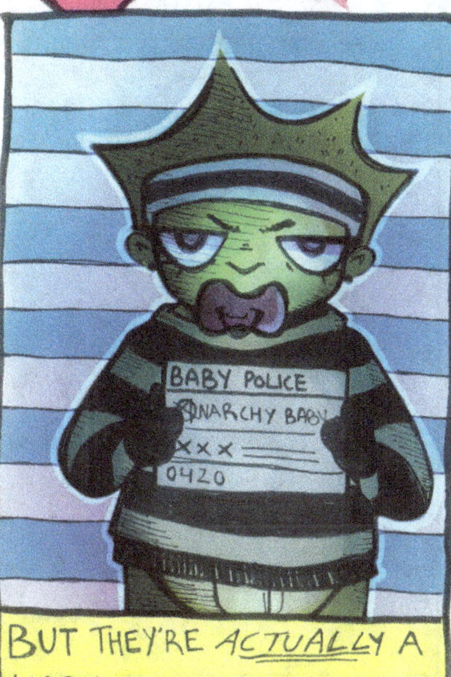

BABY POLICE
ANARCHY BABY
XXX
0420
BUT THEY'RE ACTUALLY A HARDENED CRIMINAL.

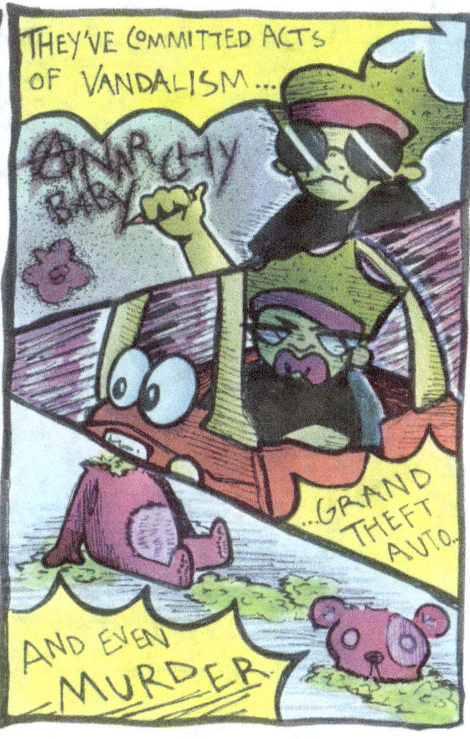

THEY'VE COMMITTED ACTS OF VANDALISM...
ANARCHY BABY
...GRAND THEFT AUTO.
AND EVEN MURDER.

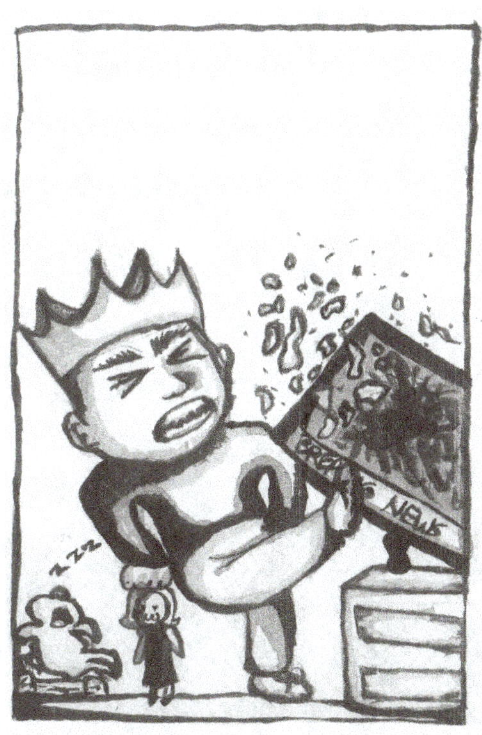

NEWS

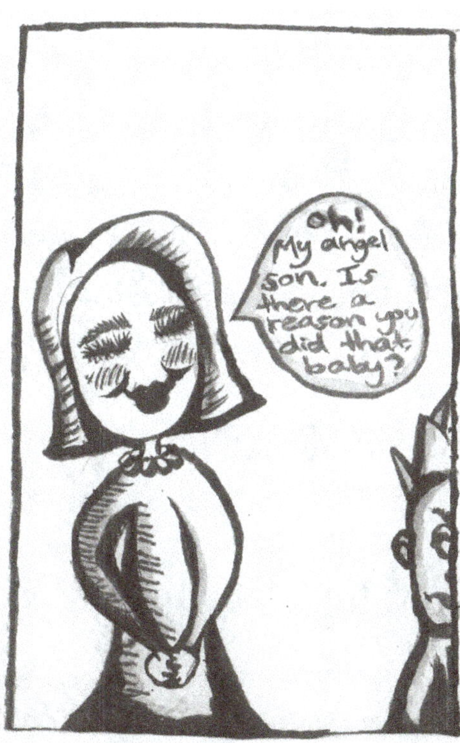

Oh! My angel son. Is there a reason you did that baby?

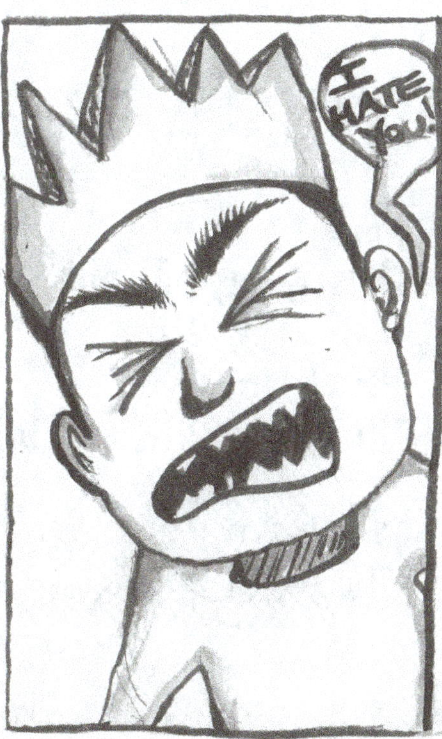

I HATE YOU!

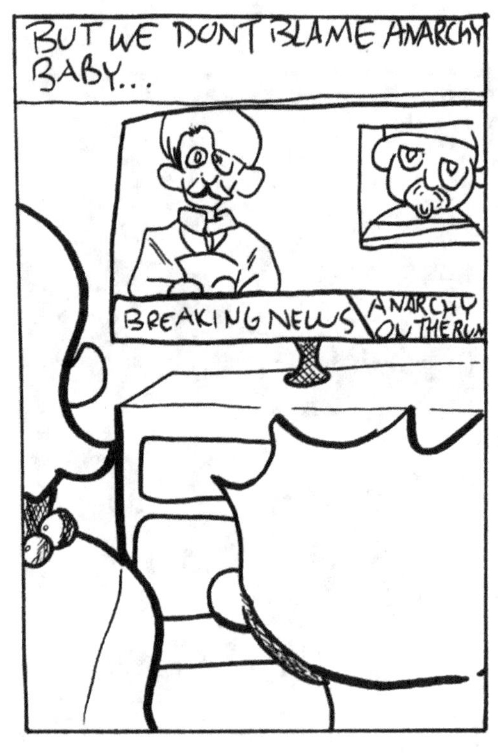

BUT WE DONT BLAME ANARCHY BABY...
BREAKING NEWS
ANARCHY ON THE RUN

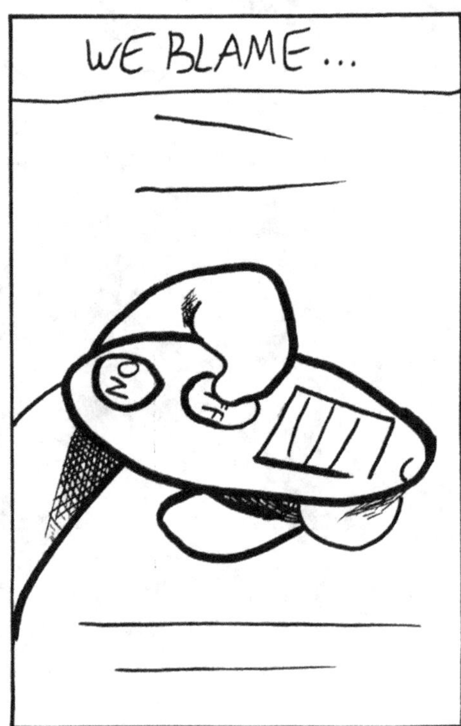

WE BLAME...

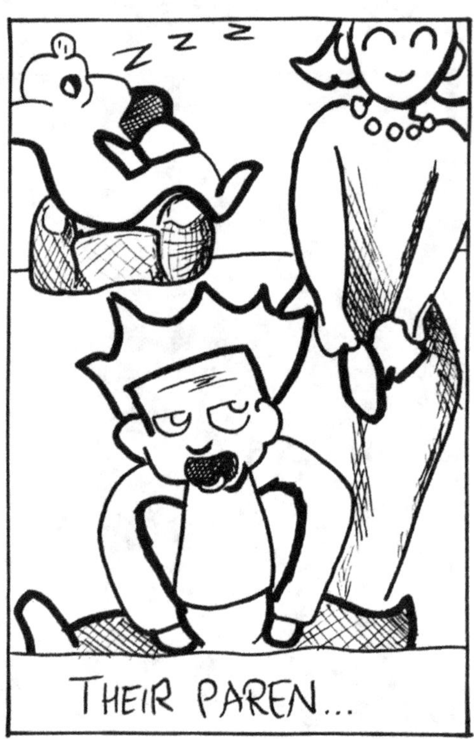

Z Z Z Z
THEIR PAREN...

ANARCHY BABY

Panels 1-3
Illustrator, Ink, and Digital Color: Casper Saez

Panels 4-6
Illustrator, Ink, and Ink Wash: Megan Hardesty

Panels 7-9
Illustrator: Theodore Fuller; Ink: Jennifer Pagan

BANANA SPLITS

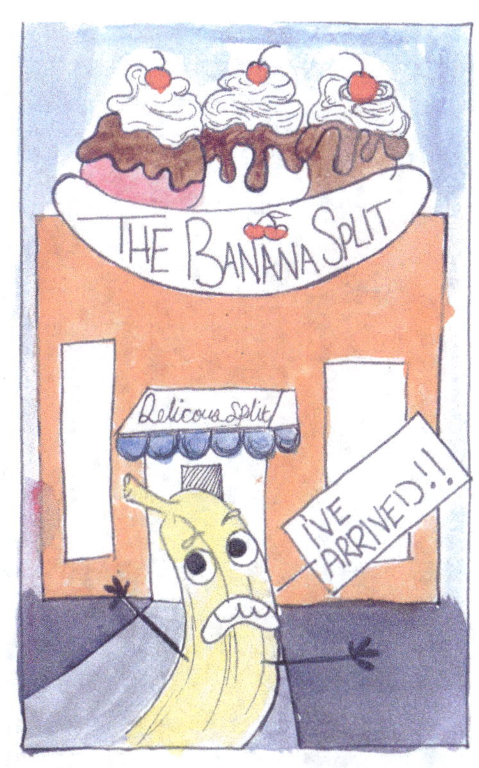

THE BANANA SPLIT
Delicous Split
I'VE ARRIVED!!

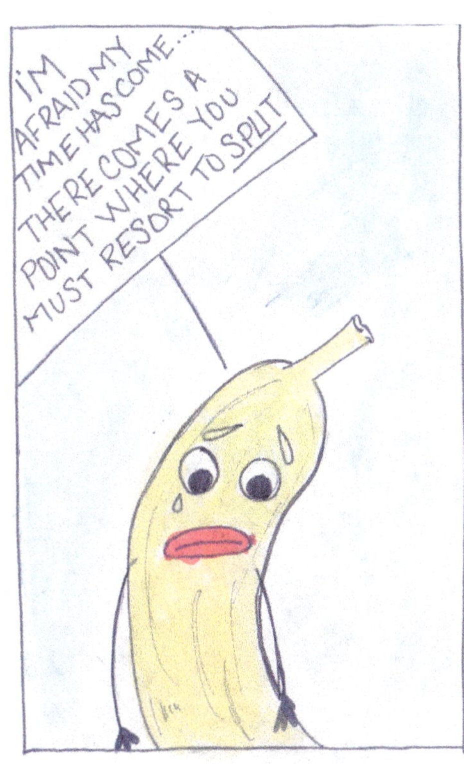

I'M AFRAID MY TIME HAS COME... THERE COMES A POINT WHERE YOU MUST RESORT TO SPLIT

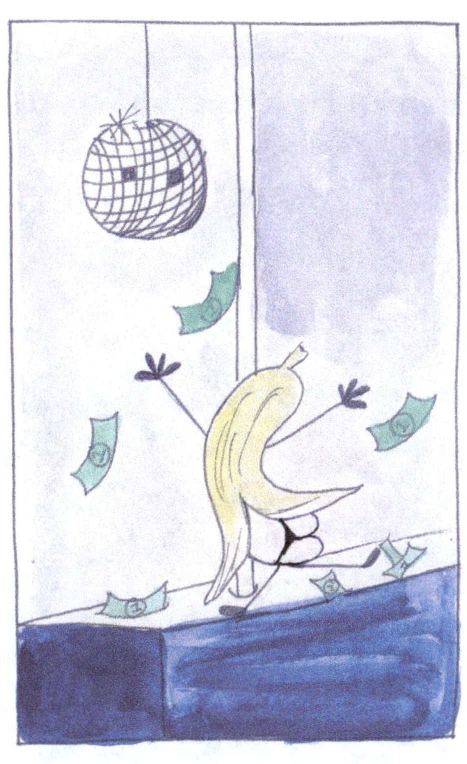

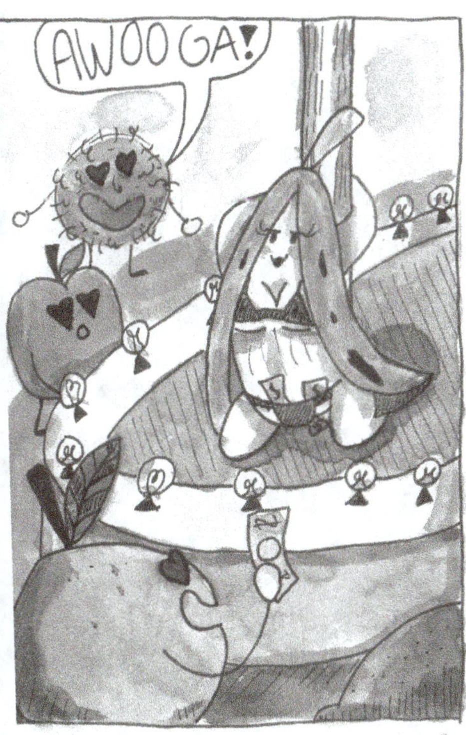

AWOOGA!

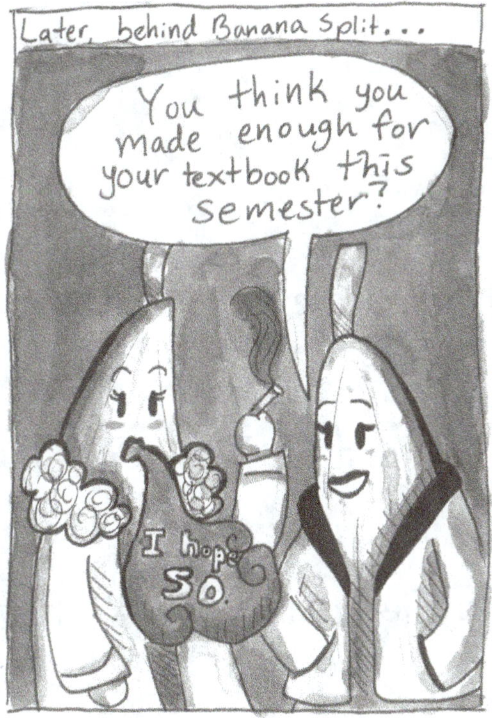

Later, behind Banana Split...
You think you made enough for your textbook this semester?
I hope so.

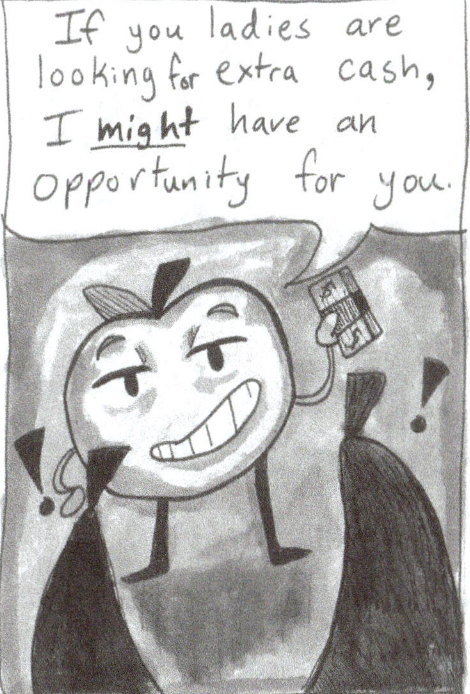

If you ladies are looking for extra cash, I might have an opportunity for you.

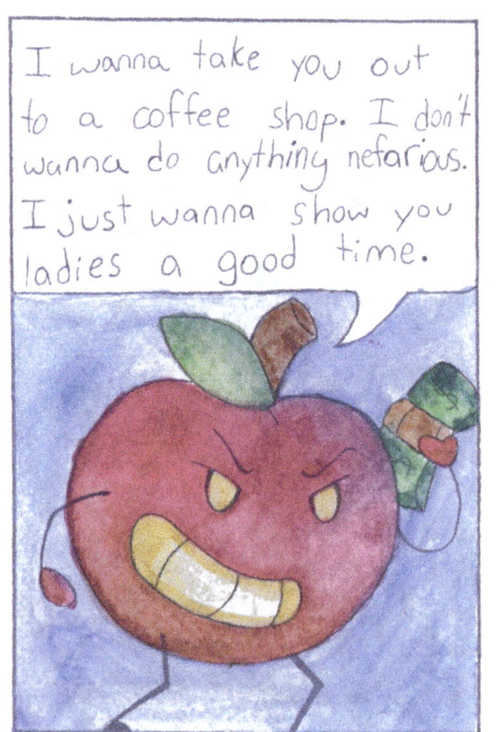

I wanna take you out to a coffee shop. I don't wanna do anything nefarious. I just wanna show you ladies a good time.

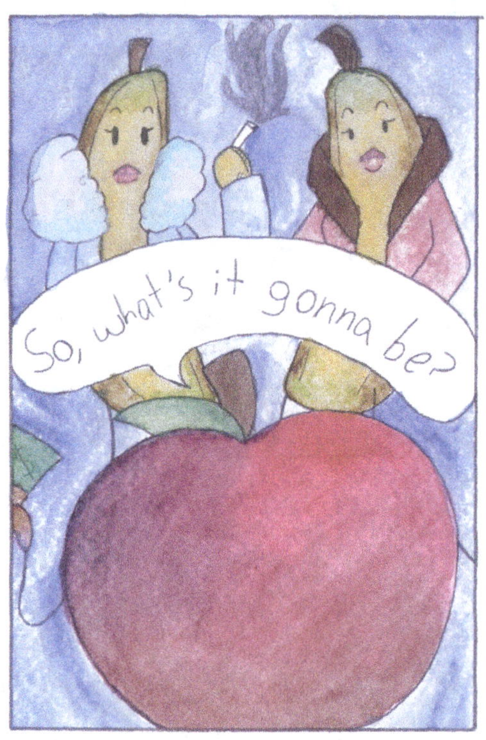

So, what's it gonna be?

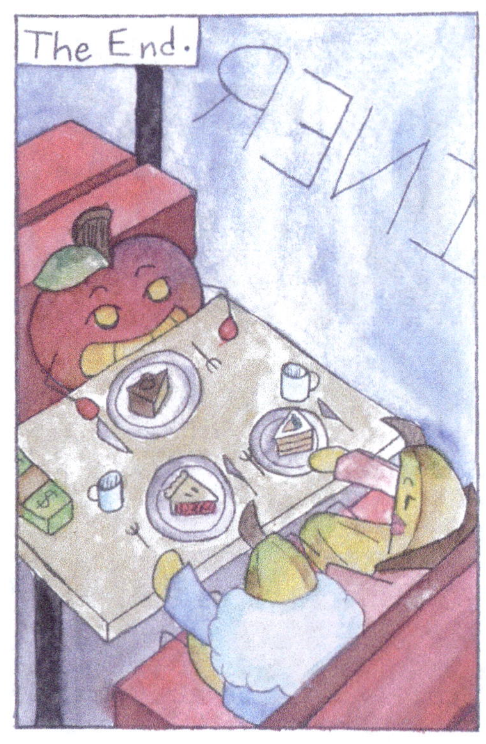

The End.

BANANA SPLiTS

Panels 1-3
Illustrator, Ink: Ayden Pigeon; Watercolor: Samantha Zarate

Panels 4-6
Illustrator: Spike Harris; Ink, and Ink Wash: Mia Jones

Panels 7-9
Illustrator and Watercolor: Kiersten Kozlowski; Ink: Nicole Kolakowski

CHASE TREE SLEEP

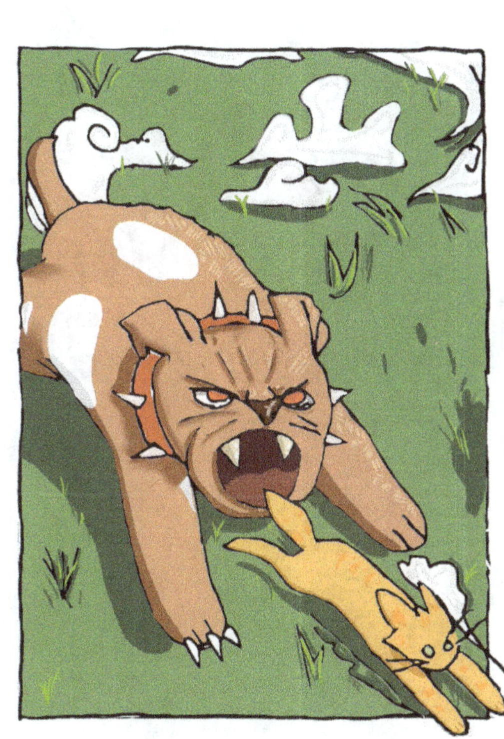

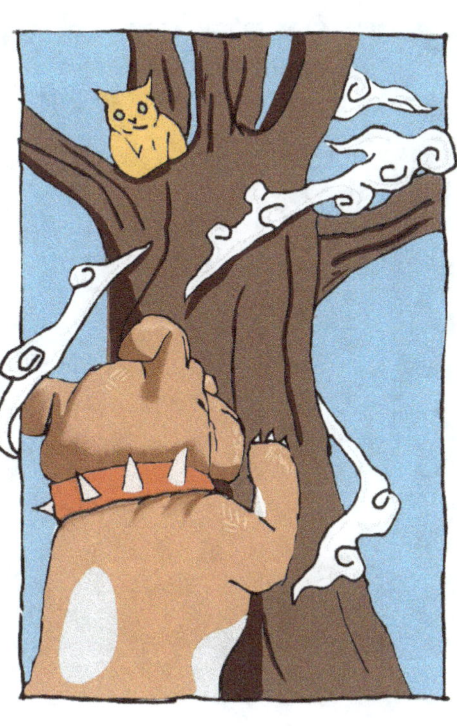

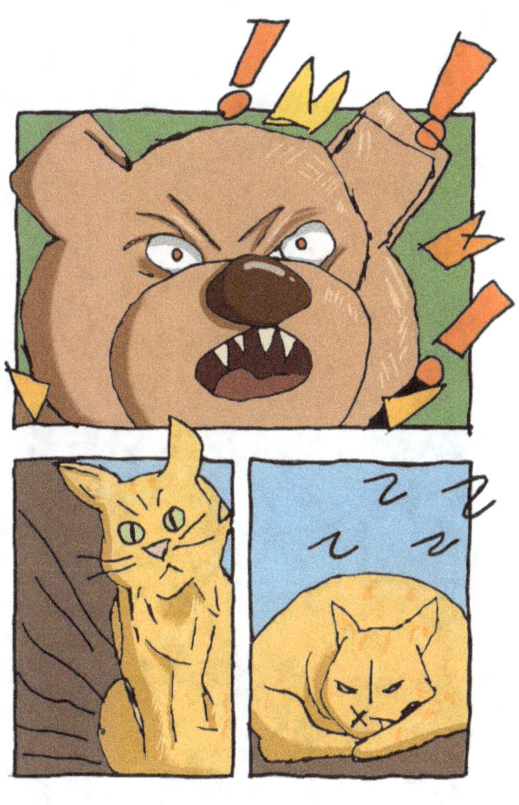

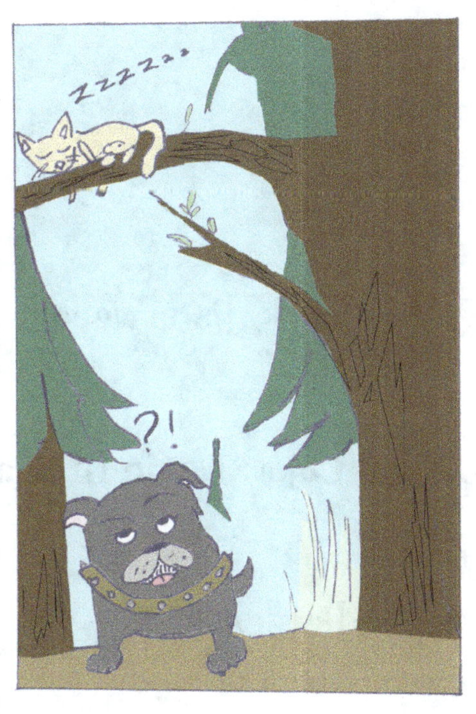

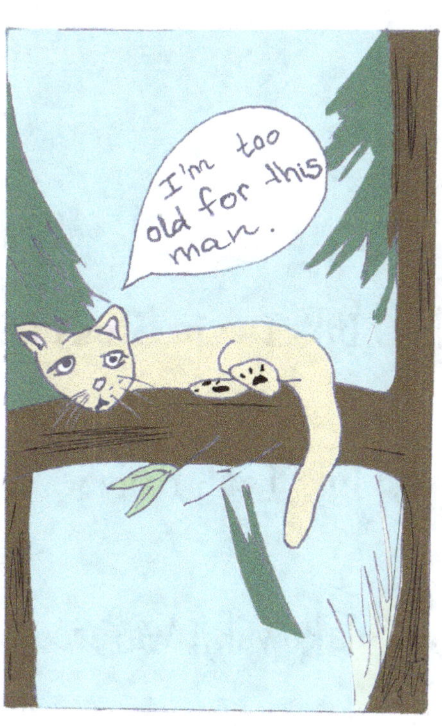

I'm too old for this man.

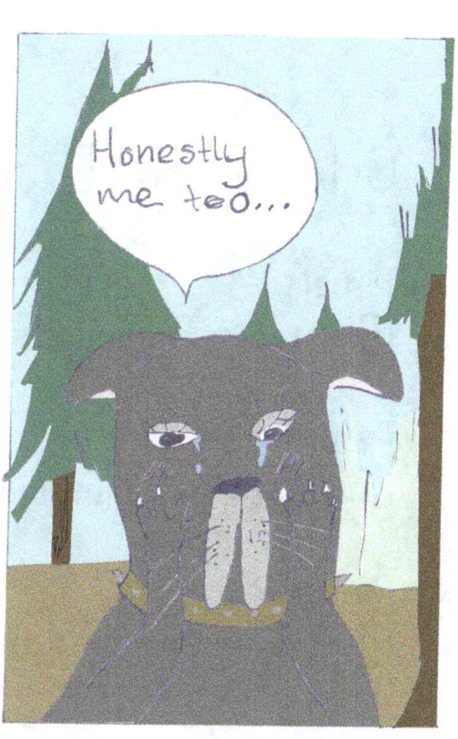

Honestly me too...

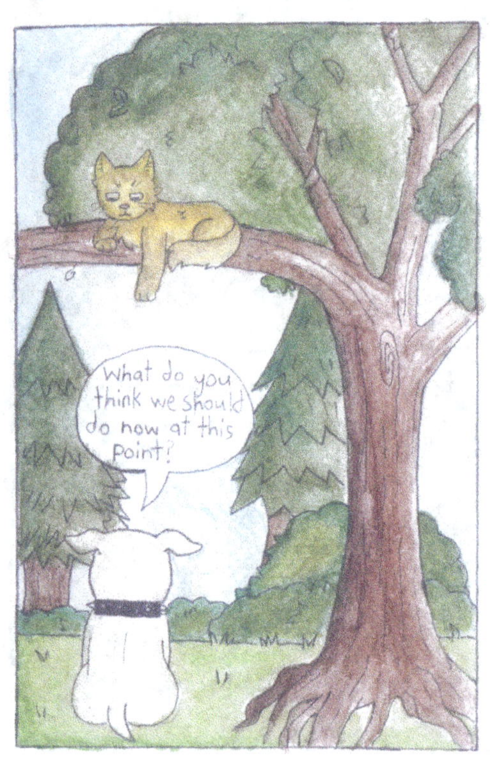

What do you think we should do now at this point?

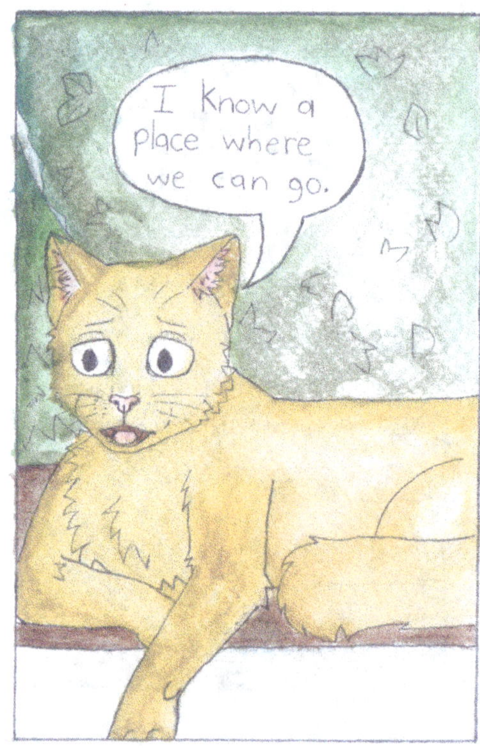

I know a place where we can go.

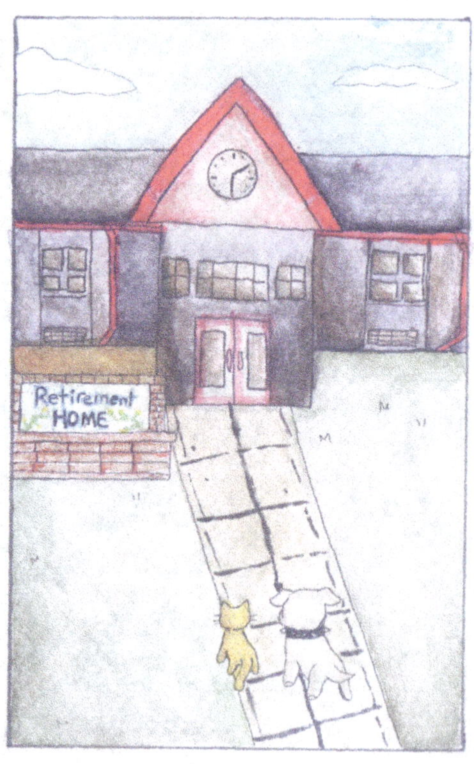

Retirement HOME

CHASE TREE SLEEP

Panels 1-3
Illustrator: Theodore Fuller; Ink: Devin Brown; Digital Color: Kalista Weed

Panels 4-6
Illustrator: Megan Hardesty; Ink: Leah Braverman; Digital Color: Devin Brown

Panels 7-9
Illustrator and Ink: Nicole Kolakowski; Watercolor: Megan Hardesty

DAPPER WEASEL CONSTRUCT

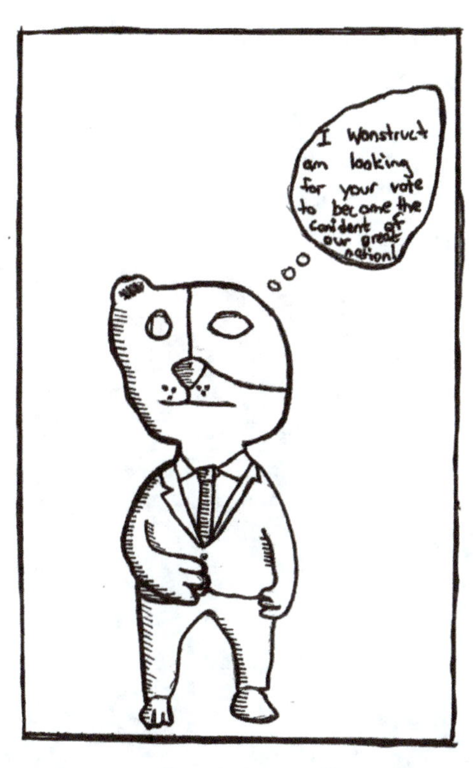

I wonstruct am looking for your vote to become the covident of our great nation!

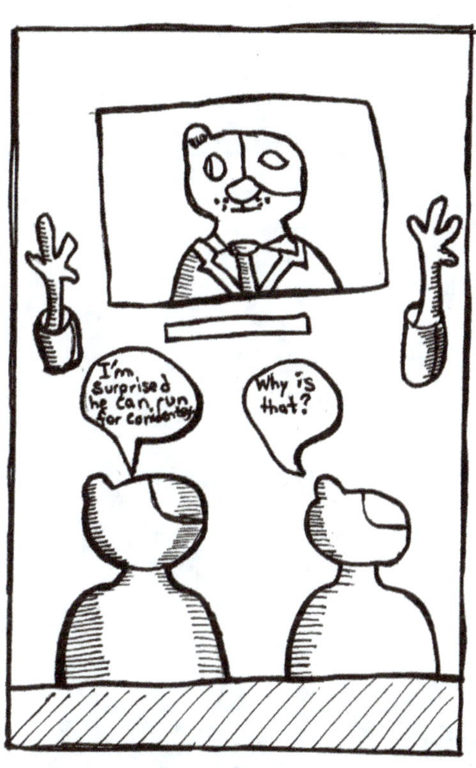

I'm surprised he can run for condentor.
Why is that?

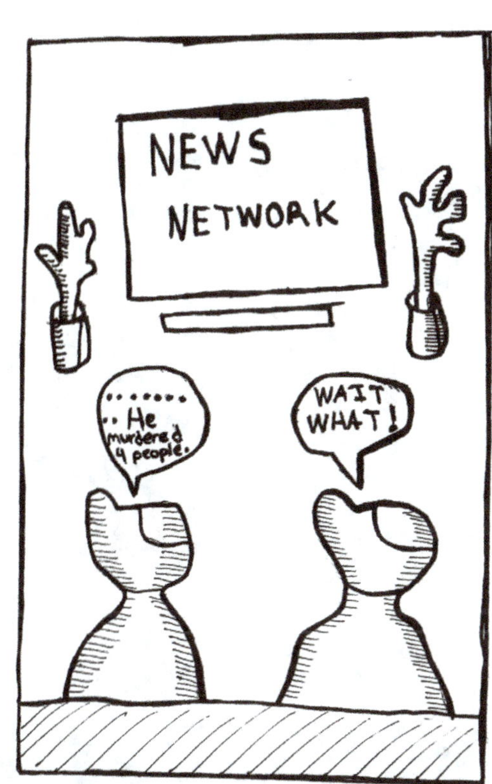

NEWS NETWORK
.. He murdered 4 people.
WAIT WHAT!

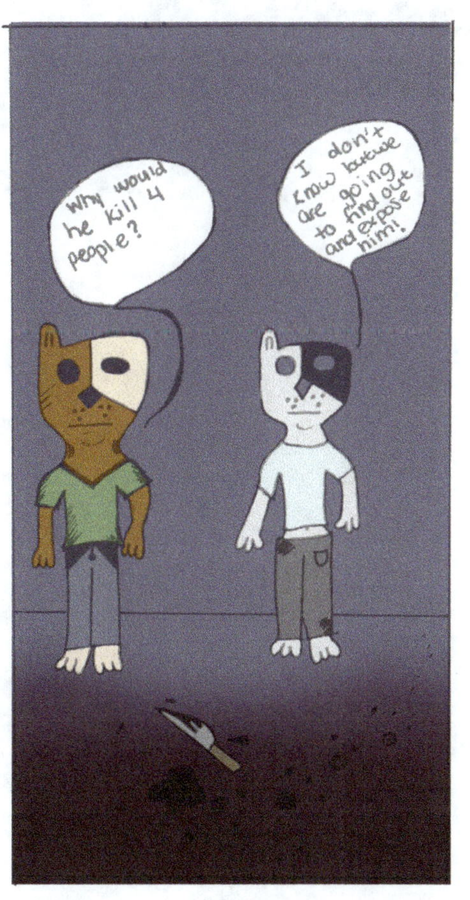

Why would he kill 4 people?
I don't know but we are going to find out and expose him!

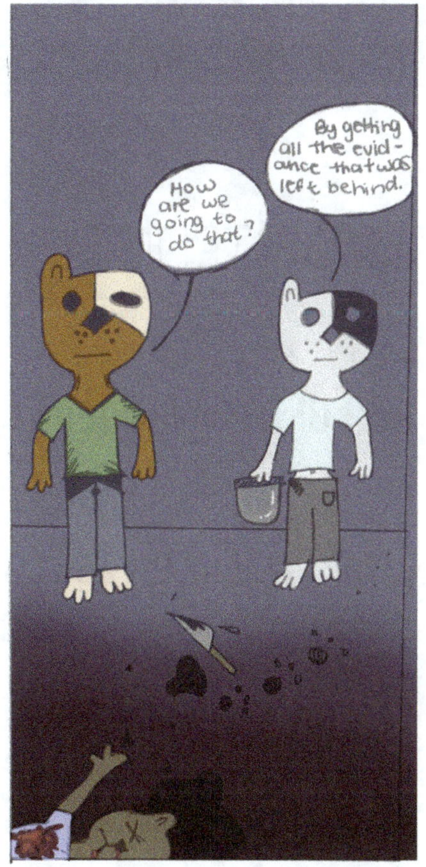

How are we going to do that?
By getting all the evidance that was left behind.

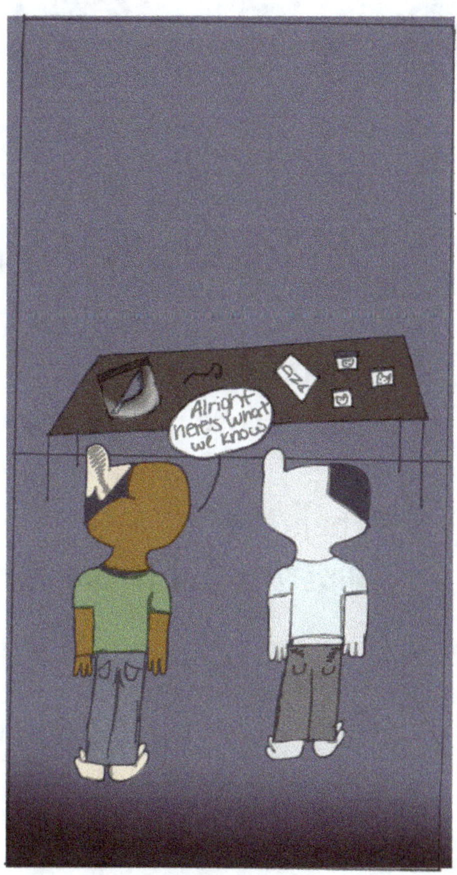

Alright here's what we know.

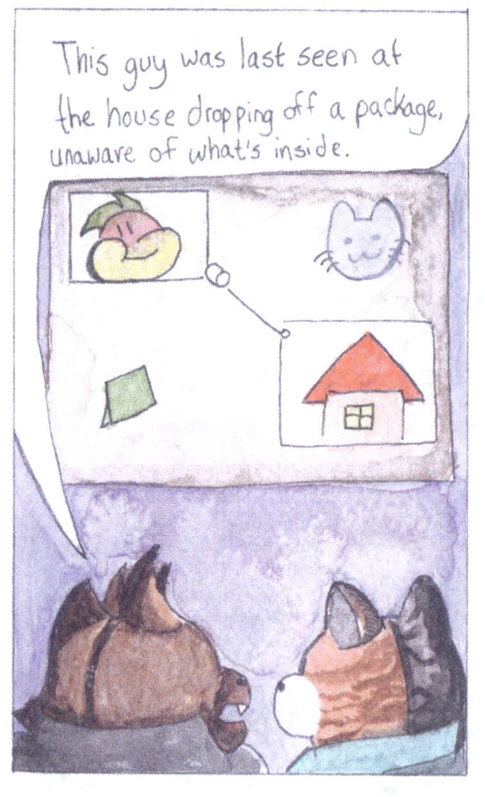

This guy was last seen at the house dropping off a package, unaware of what's inside.

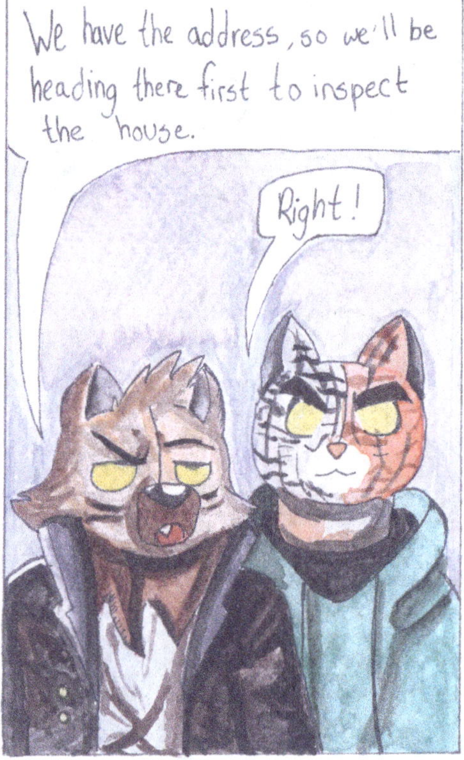

We have the address, so we'll be heading there first to inspect the house.
Right!

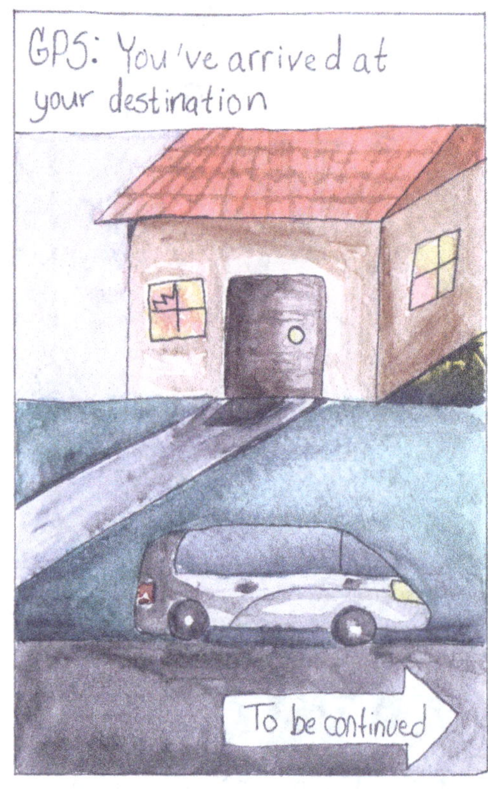

GPS: You've arrived at your destination
To be continued

DAPPER WEASEL CONSTRUCT

Panels 1-3
Illustrator: Devin Brown; Ink: Christopher Light

Panels 4-6
Illustrator: Tianne Murray, Ink: Ayden Pigeon; Digital Color: Alina Jones

Panels 7-9
Illustrator: Christopher Light; Ink: Mason Higgins; Watercolor: Jennifer Pagan

DOG DAYS

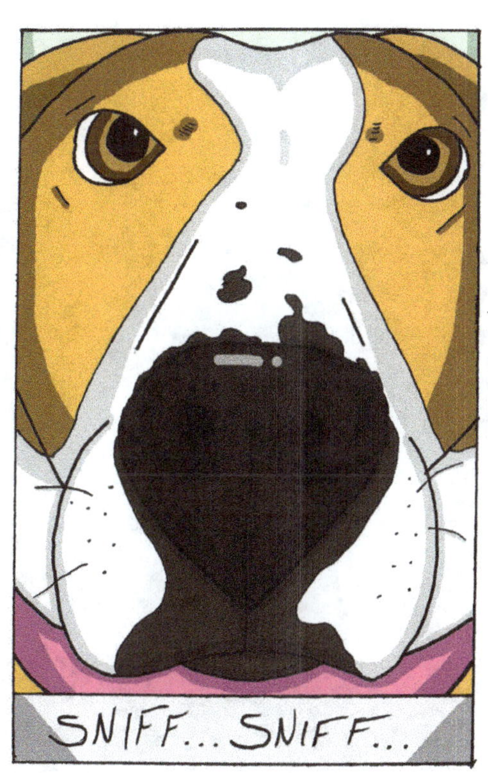

SNIFF... SNIFF...

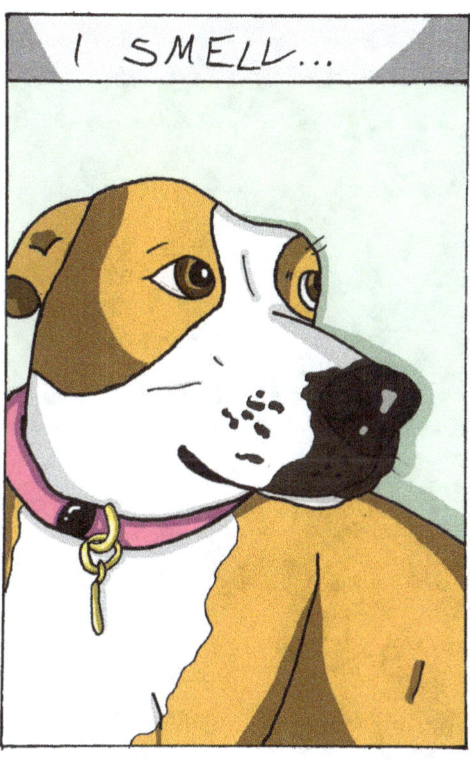

I SMELL...

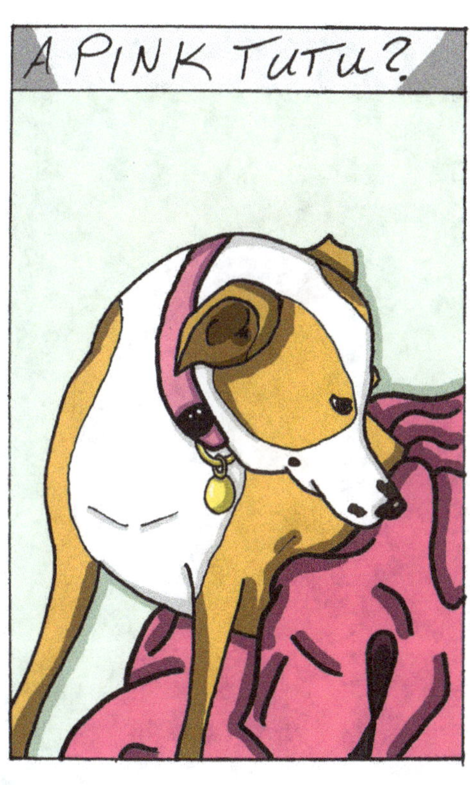

A PINK TUTU?

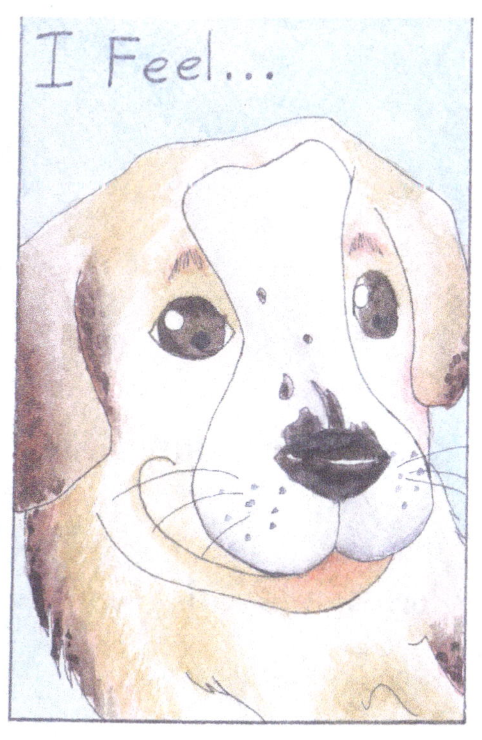

I Feel...

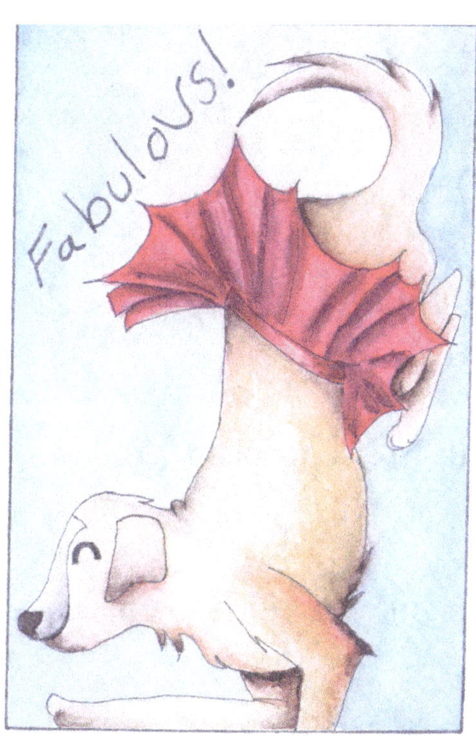

Fabulous!

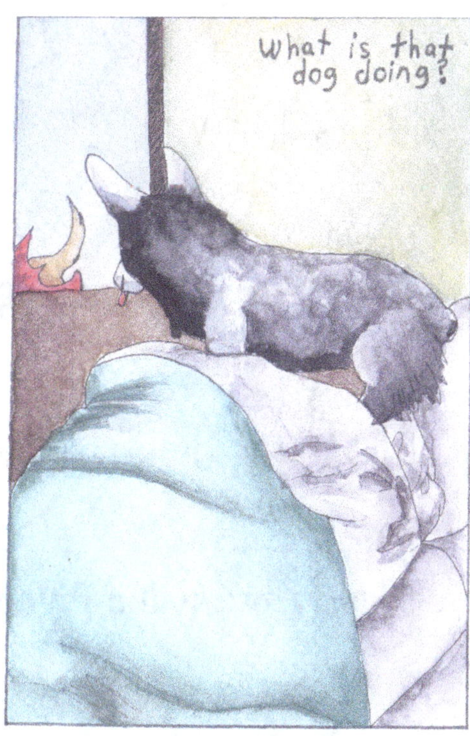

What is that dog doing?

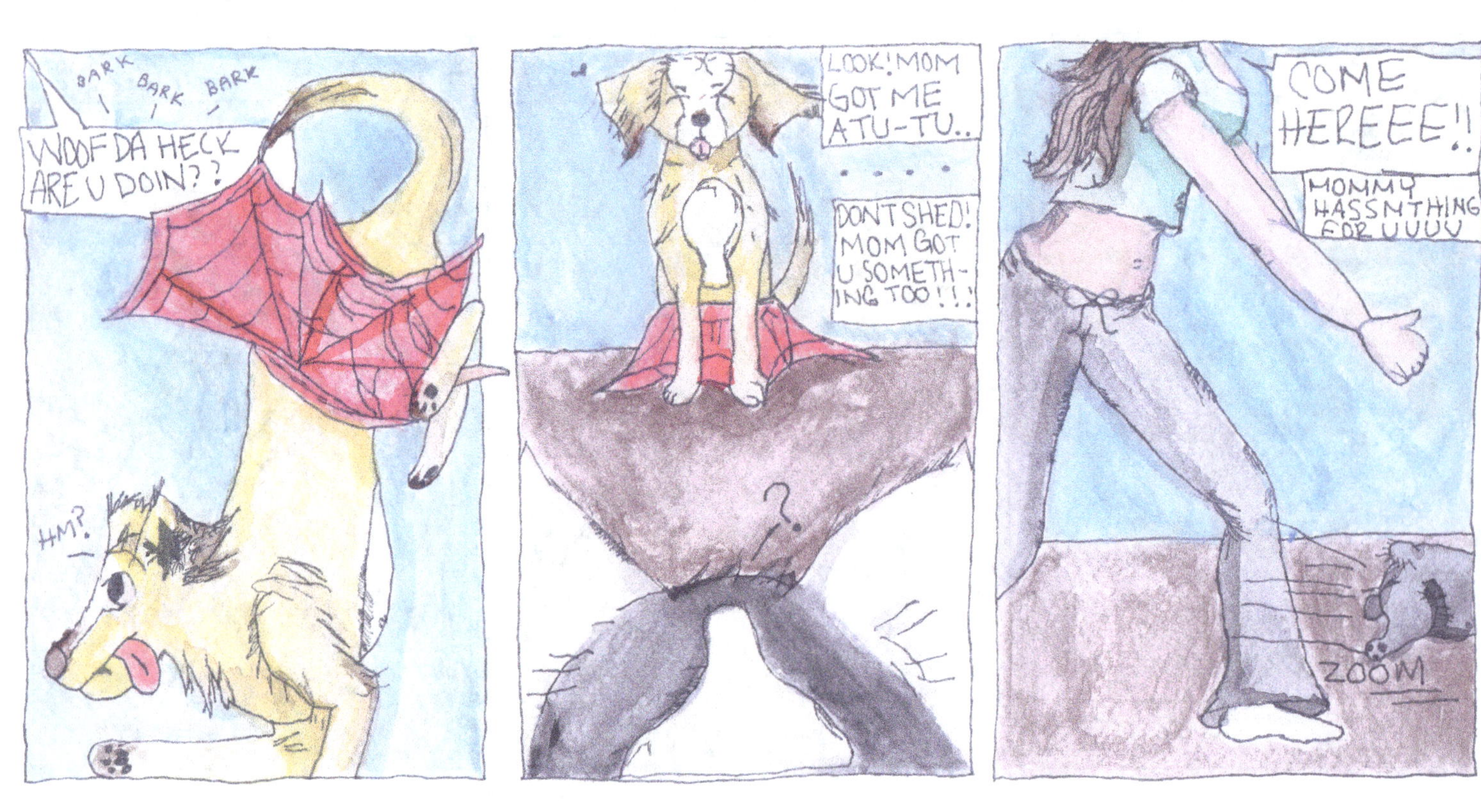

BARK BARK BARK
WOOF DA HECK ARE U DOIN??
HM?
LOOK! MOM GOT ME A TU-TU..
DONT SHED! MOM GOT U SOMETH-ING TOO!!!
?
COME HEREEE!!
MOMMY HASS NTHING FOR UUUU
ZOOM

DOG DAYS

Panels 1-3
Illustrator, Ink, and Digital Color: Emily Brier

Panels 4-6
Illustrator: Jenifer Pagan; Ink: Kiersten Kozlowski; Watercolor: Emily Brier

Panels 7-9
Illustrator: Ayden Pigeon; Ink: Devin Brown; Watercolor: Nicole Kolakowski

EDUARDO THE CARPENTER

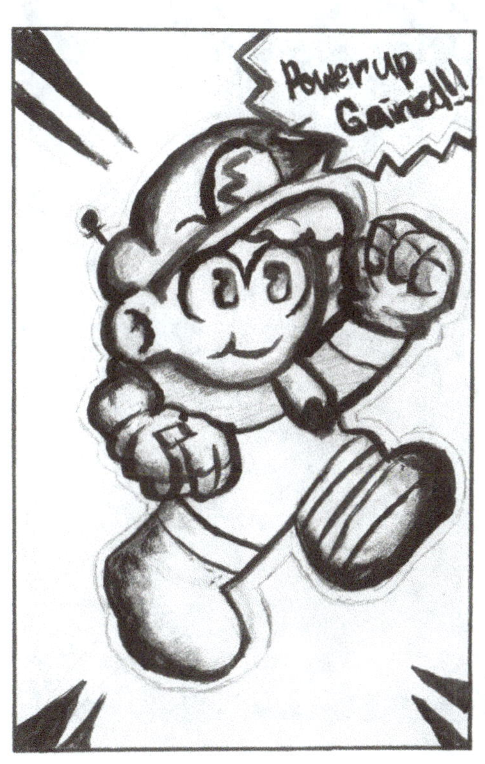

Power up
Gained!!

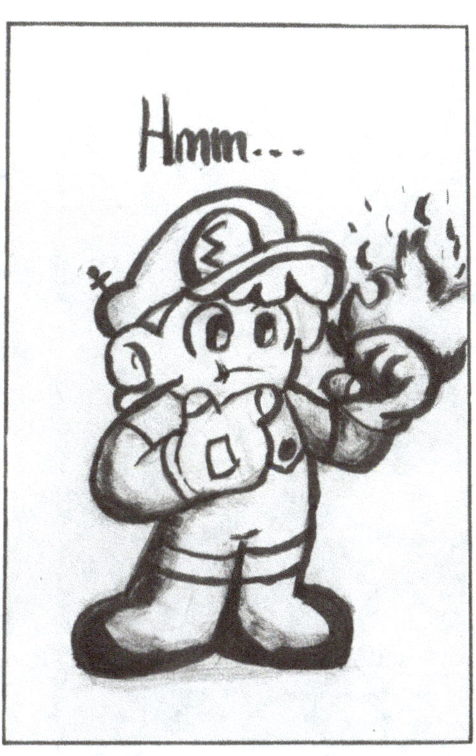

Hmm...

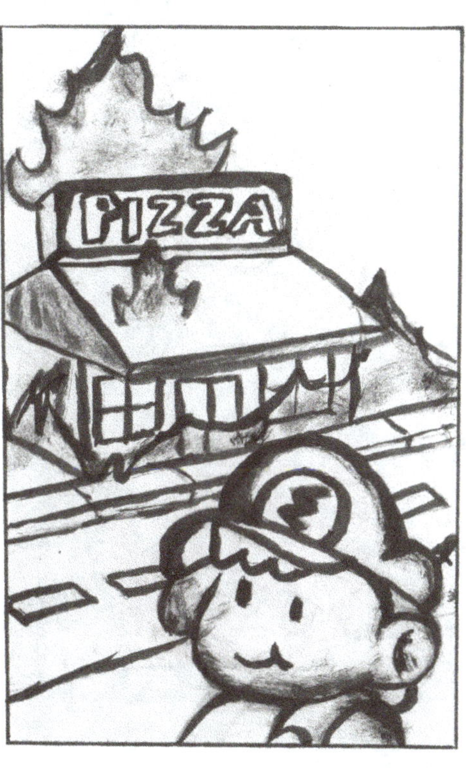

PIZZA

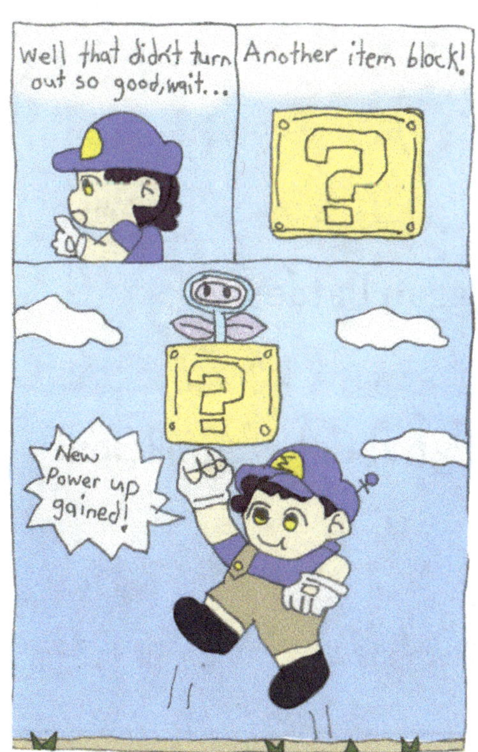

Well that didn't turn out so good, wait...
Another item block!
New Power up gained!

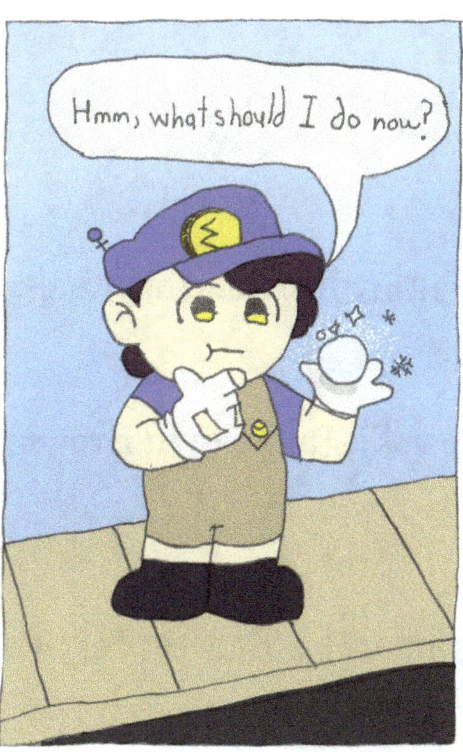

Hmm, what should I do now?

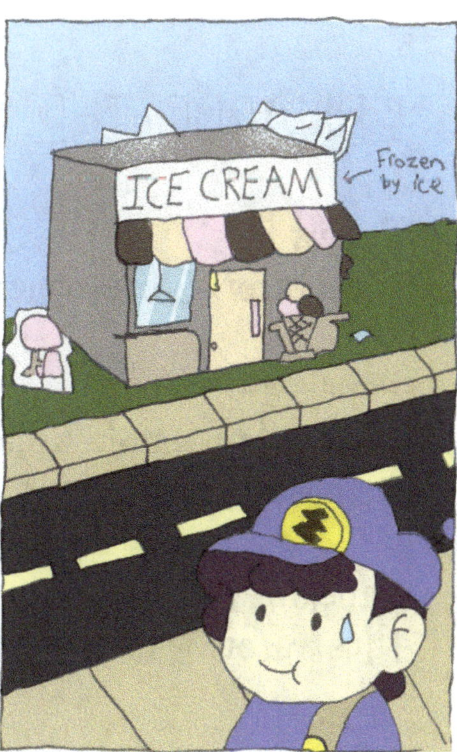

ICE CREAM
Frozen by ice

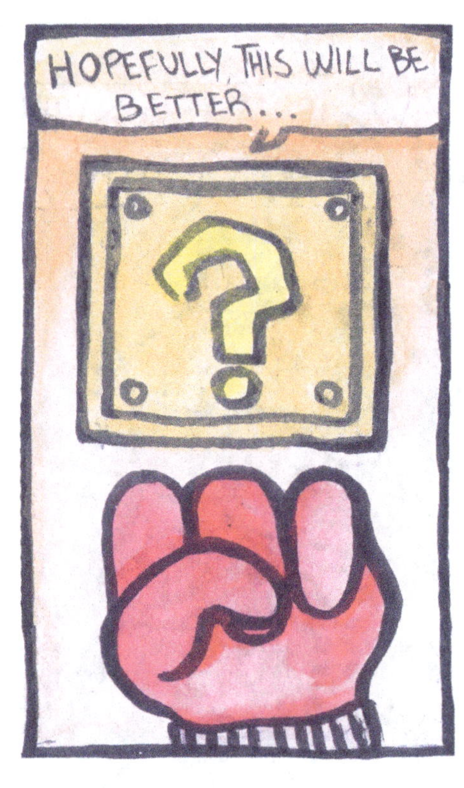

HOPEFULLY, THIS WILL BE BETTER...

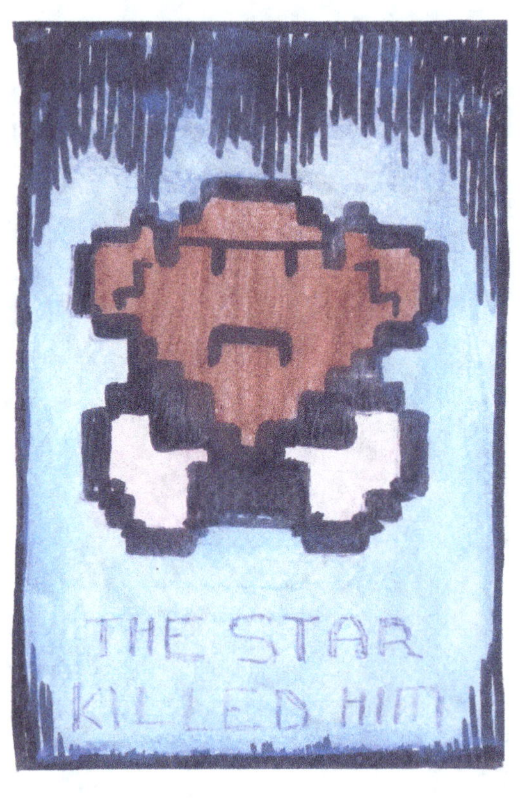

THE STAR KILLED HIM

EDUARDO THE CARPENTER

Panels 1-3
Illustrator: Christopher Light; Ink and Ink Wash: Megan Hardesty

Panels 4-6
Illustrator: Nicole Kolakowski; Ink; Devin Brown; Digital Color: Alina Jones Dempsey Langan

Panels 7-9
Illustrator, Watercolor: Samantha Zarate; Ink: Casper Saez

GAY MEDIEVAL WEDDING

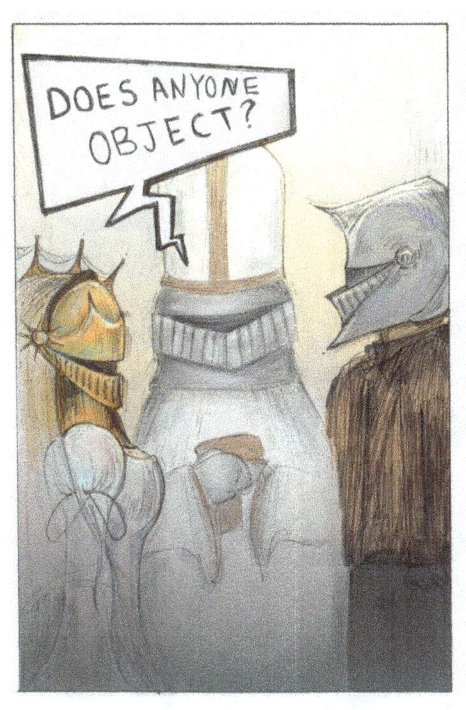

DOES ANYONE OBJECT?

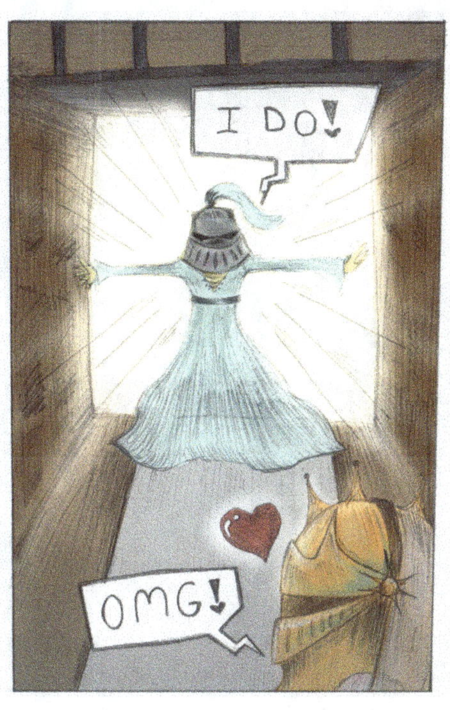

I DO!
OMG!

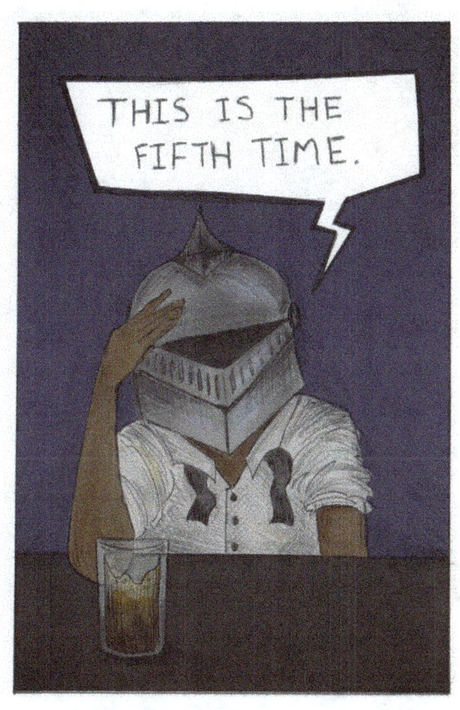

THIS IS THE FIFTH TIME.

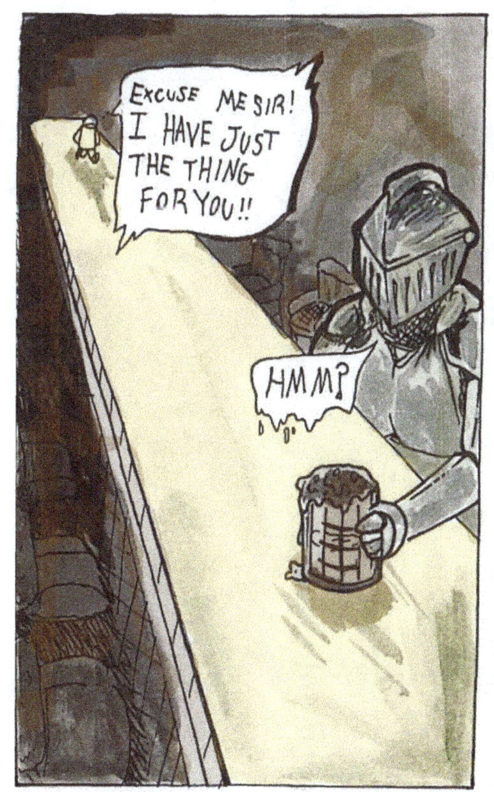

EXCUSE ME SIR! I HAVE JUST THE THING FOR YOU!!
HMM?

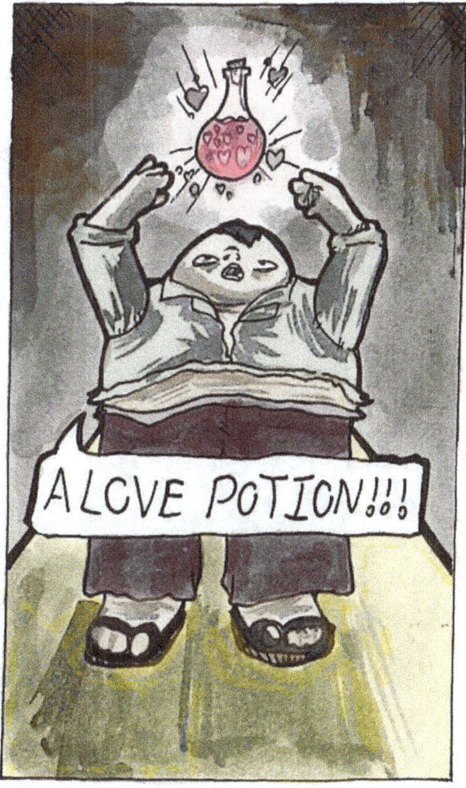

A LOVE POTION!!!

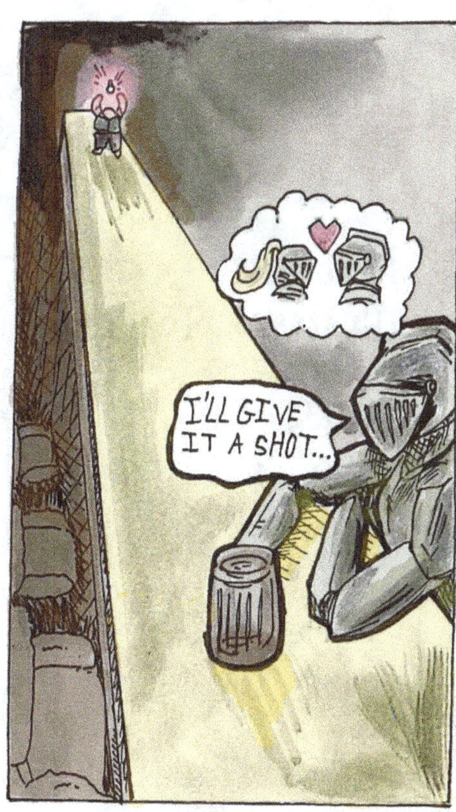

I'LL GIVE IT A SHOT...

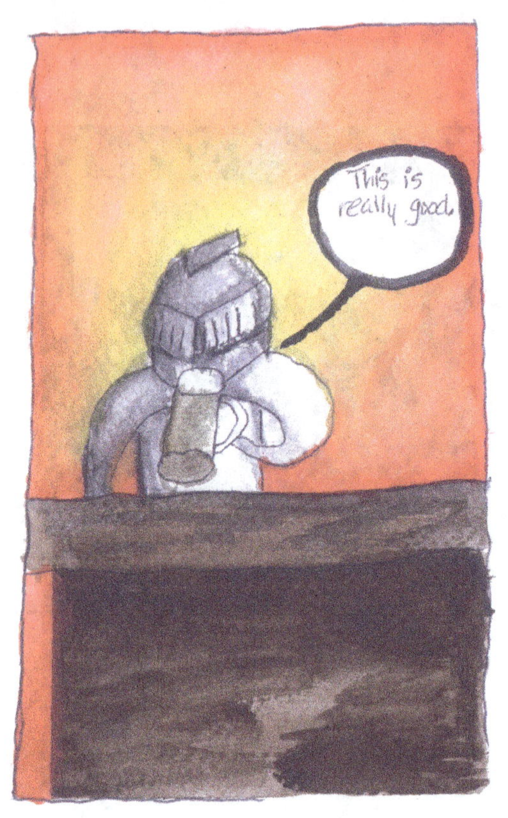

This is really good.

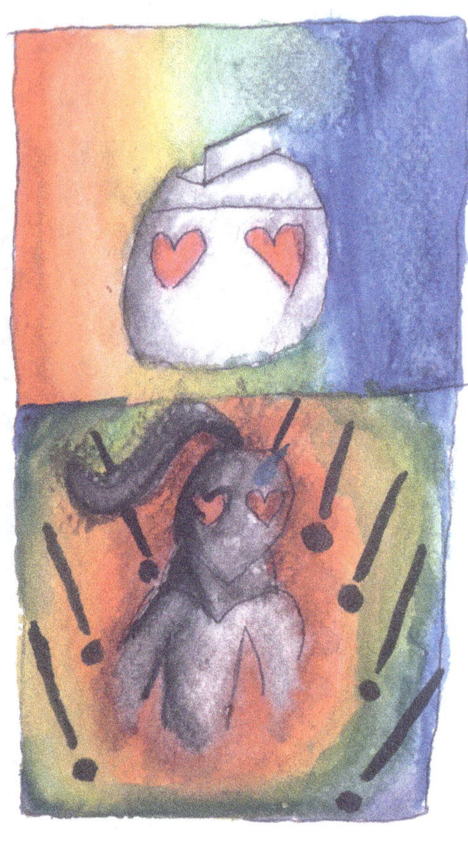

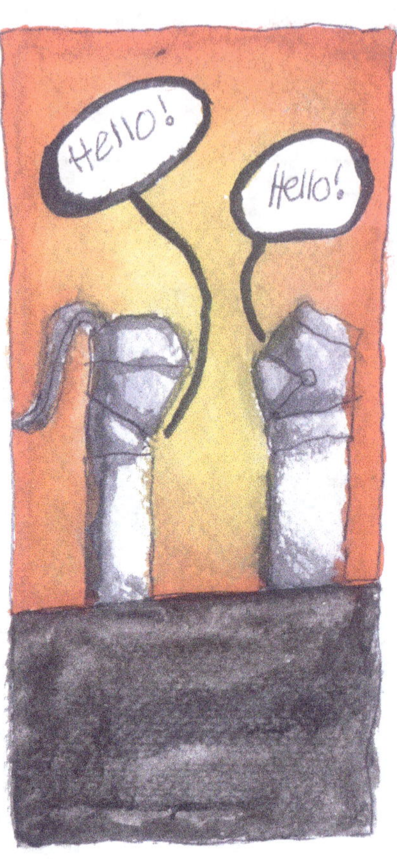

Hello!
Hello!

GAY MEDIEVAL WEDDING

Panels 1-3
Illustrator, Ink, and Digital Color: Brianna Vongmany

Panels 4-6
Illustrator, Digital Color: Dempsey Langan; Ink: Alina Jones;
Ink Wash: Brianna Vongmany

Panels 7-9
Illustrator, Ink: Tianne Murray; Watercolor: Megan Hardesty

INFINITE SUNSHINE

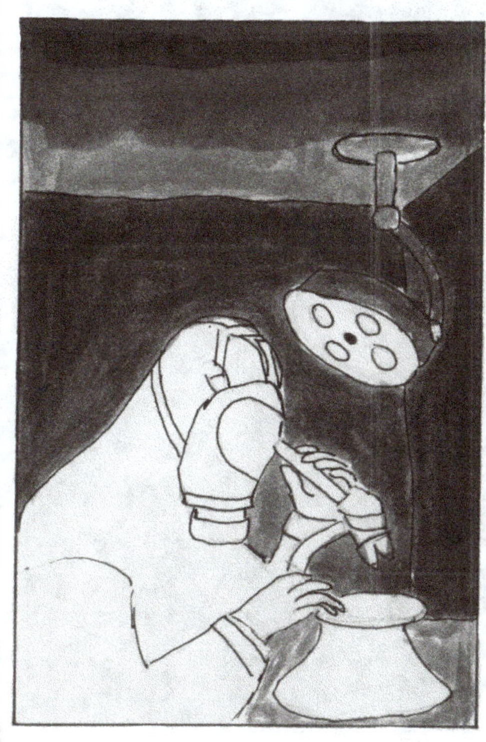

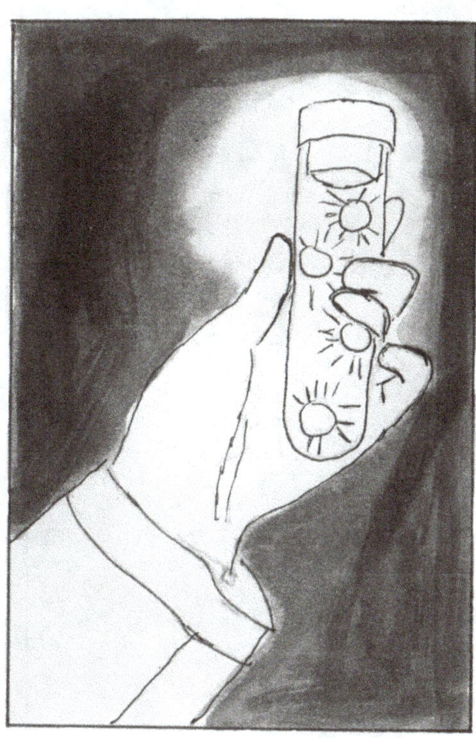

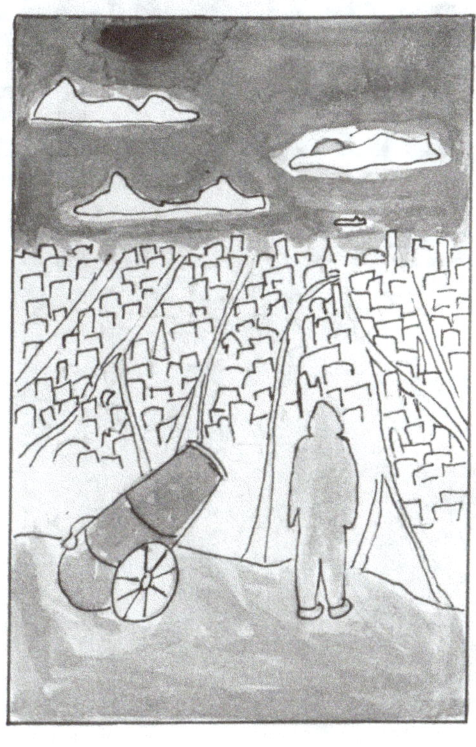

INFINITE SUNSHINE
CONTINUED →

INFINITE SUN·VID

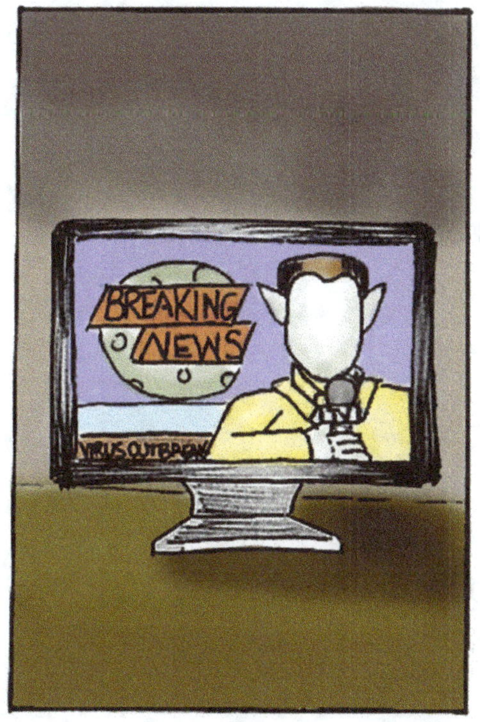
BREAKING NEWS
VIRUS OUTBREAK

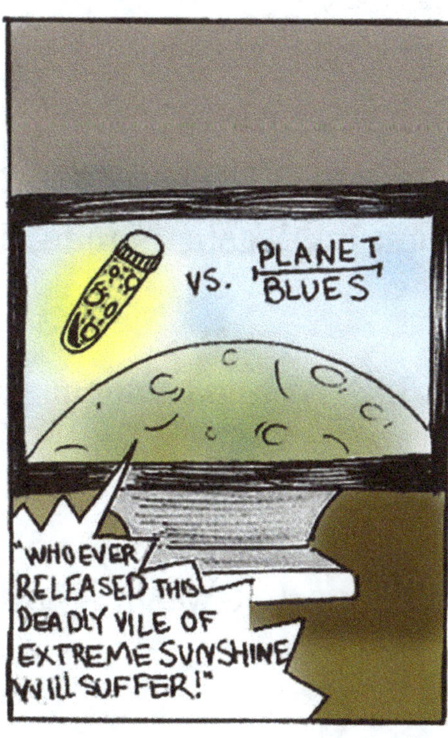
VS. PLANET BLUES
"WHO EVER RELEASED THIS DEADLY VILE OF EXTREME SUNSHINE WILL SUFFER!"

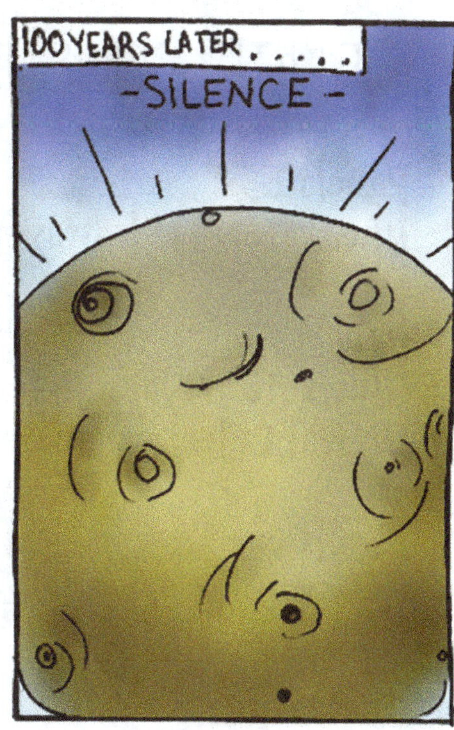
100 YEARS LATER......
- SILENCE -

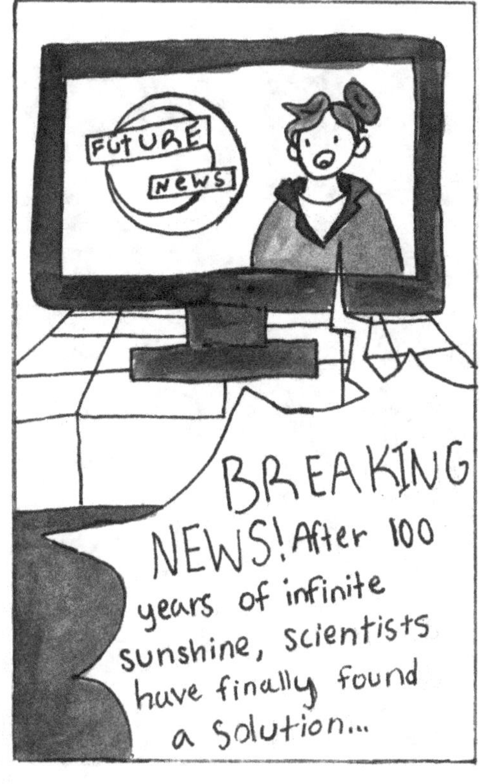

FUTURE NEWS
BREAKING NEWS! After 100 years of infinite sunshine, scientists have finally found a solution...

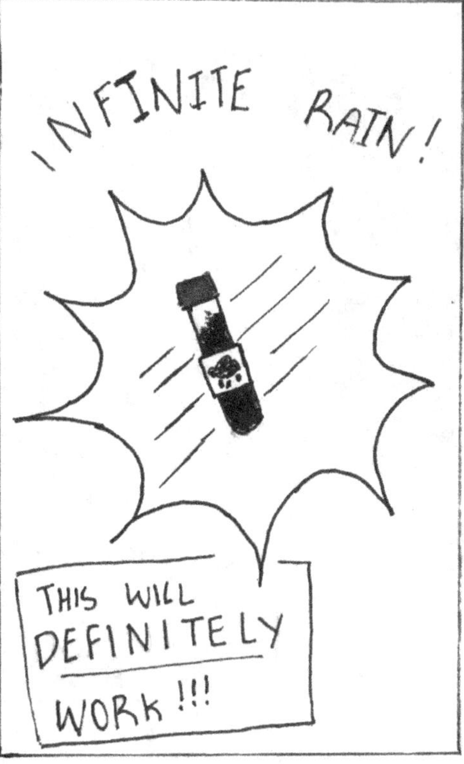

INFINITE RAIN!
THIS WILL DEFINITELY WORK!!!

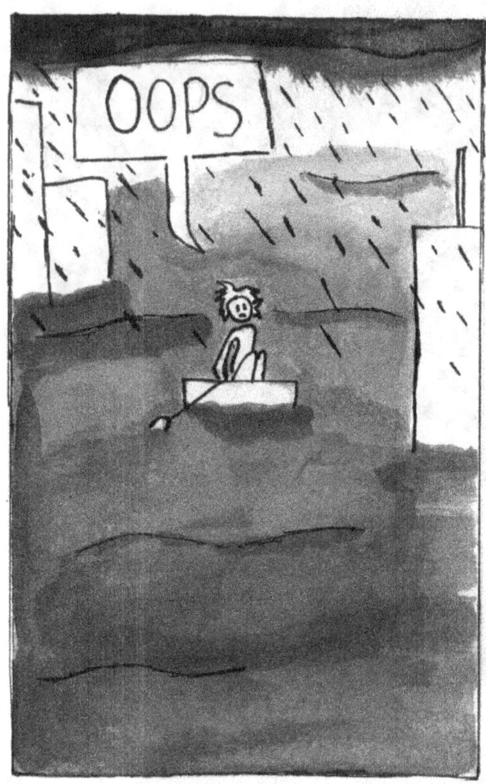

OOPS

iNFiNiTE SUNSHiNE

Panels 1-3
Illustrator: Leah Braverman; Ink Wash: Tianne Murray

Panels 4-6
Illustrator: Ayden Pigeon; Ink: Brianna Vongmany;
Digital Color: Leah Braverman

Panels 7-9
Illustrator: Casper Saez; Ink and Ink Wash: Ryan Ackerman

MAMA MIA

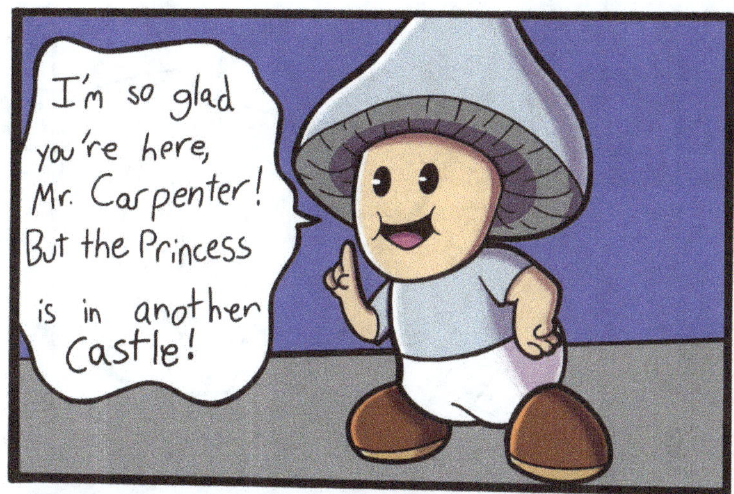

I'm so glad you're here, Mr. Carpenter! But the Princess is in another Castle!

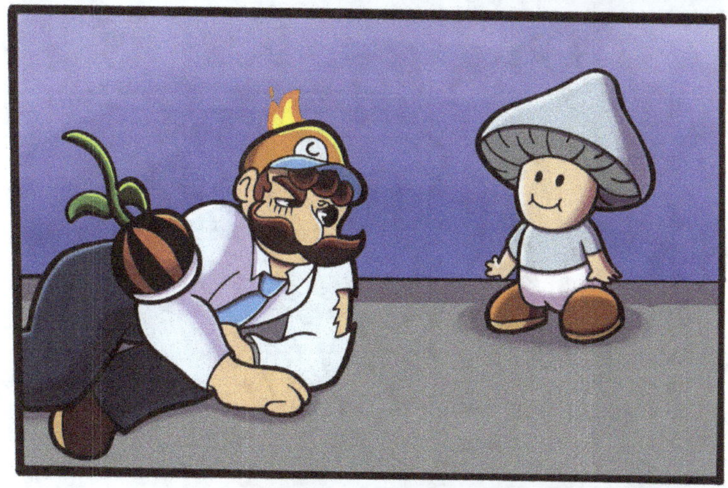

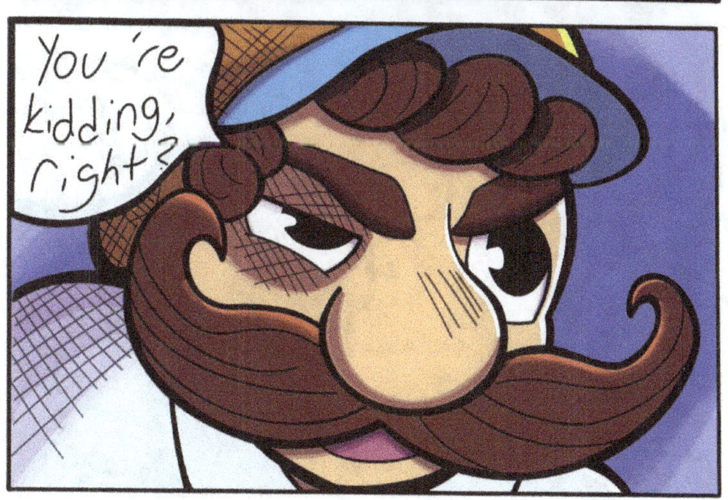

You're kidding, right?

Panels 1-3
Illustrator: Kiersten Kozlowski; Ink and Ink Wash: Spike Harris;
Digital Color: Christopher Light

MAMA MiA

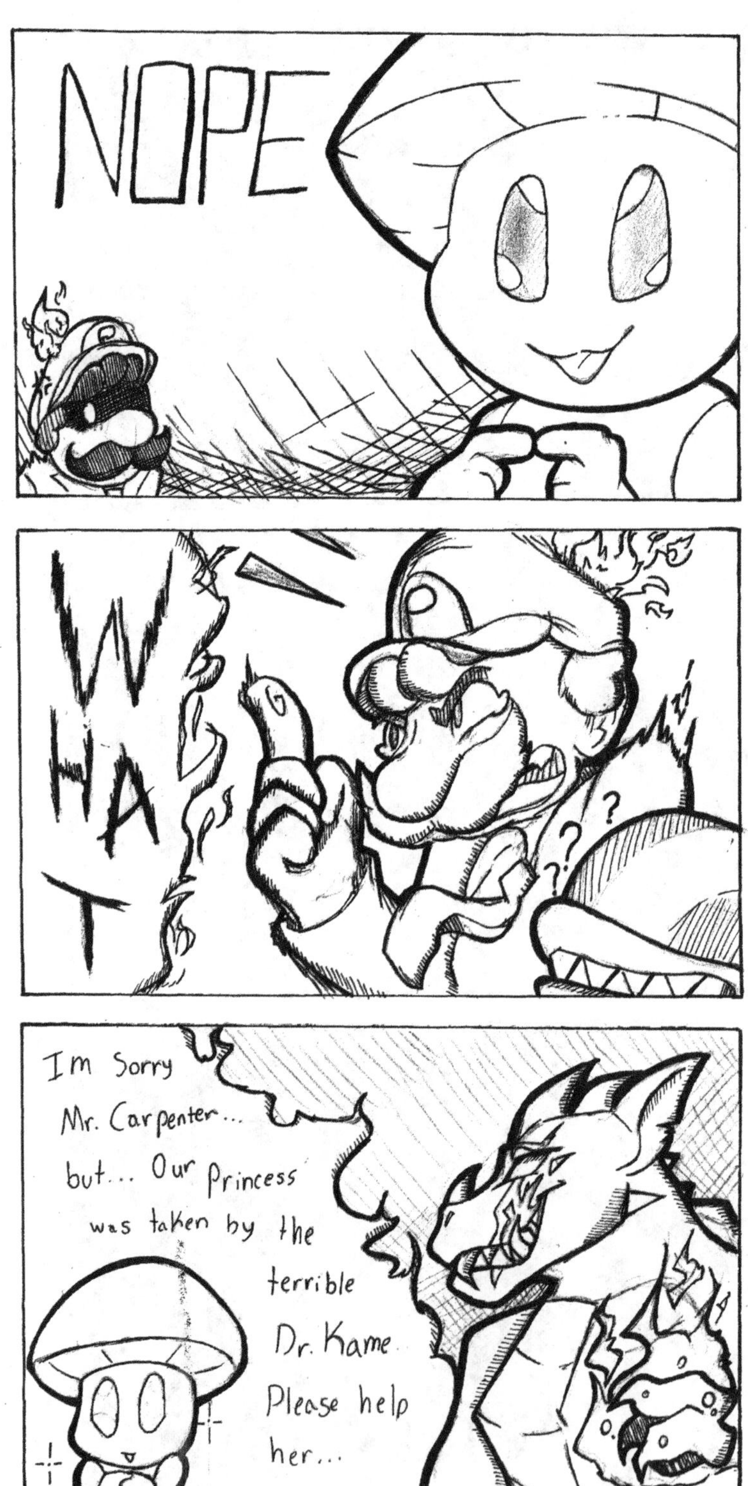

NOPE

WHAT

I'm sorry
Mr. Carpenter...
but... Our princess
was taken by the
terrible
Dr. Kame.
Please help
her...

Panels 4-6
Illustrator: Alina Jones; Ink: Christopher Light

MAMA MIA

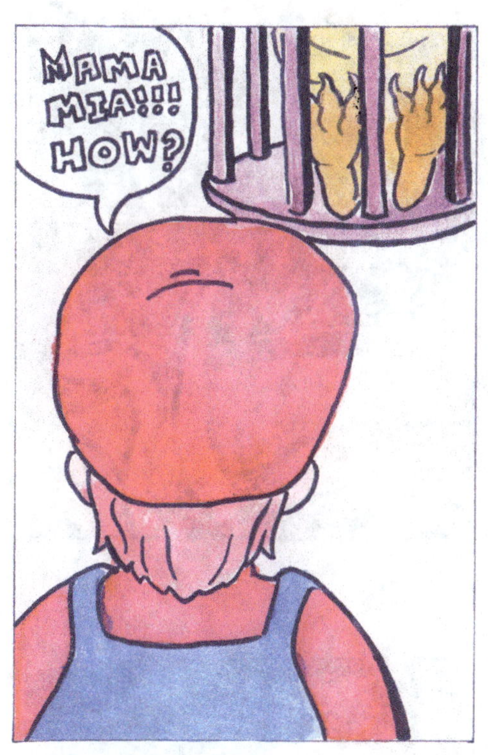

MAMA MIA!!! HOW?

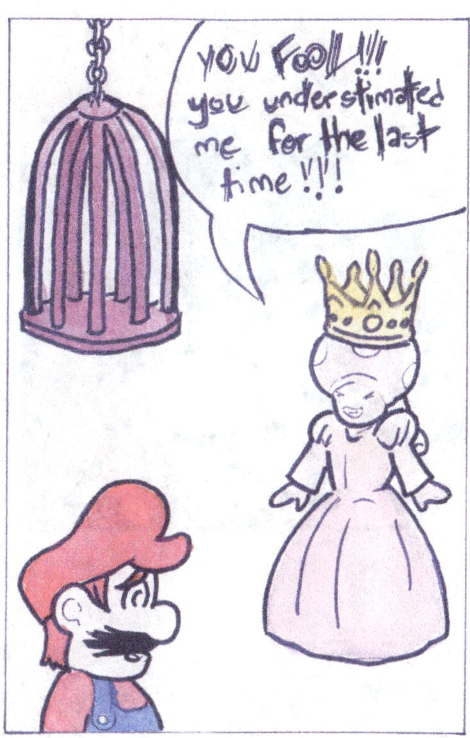

YOU FOOL!!! you underestimated me for the last time !!!!

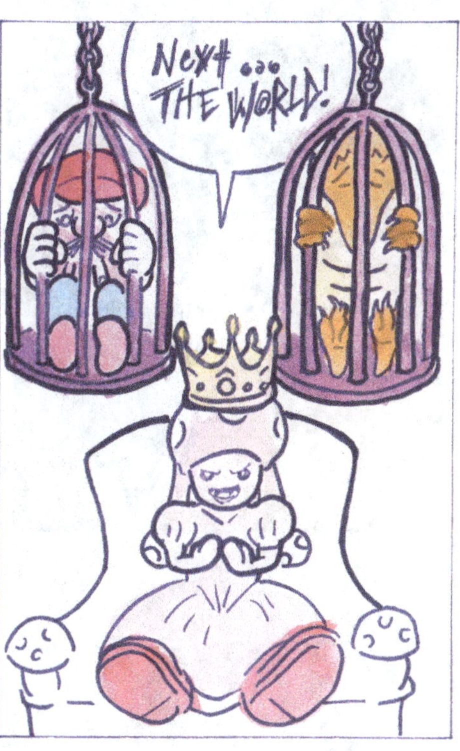

NEXT... THE WORLD!

Panels 7-9
Illustrator: Leah Braverman; Ink and Watercolor: Theodore Fuller

MARiCOLOUS ZEGEiNE CERAUNOGRAPH

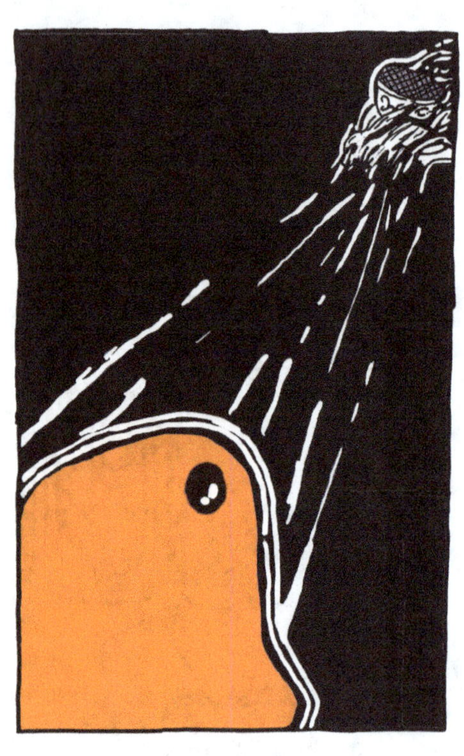
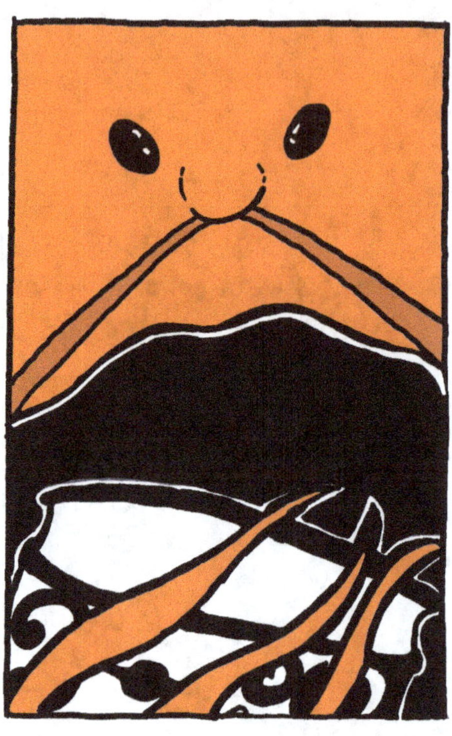
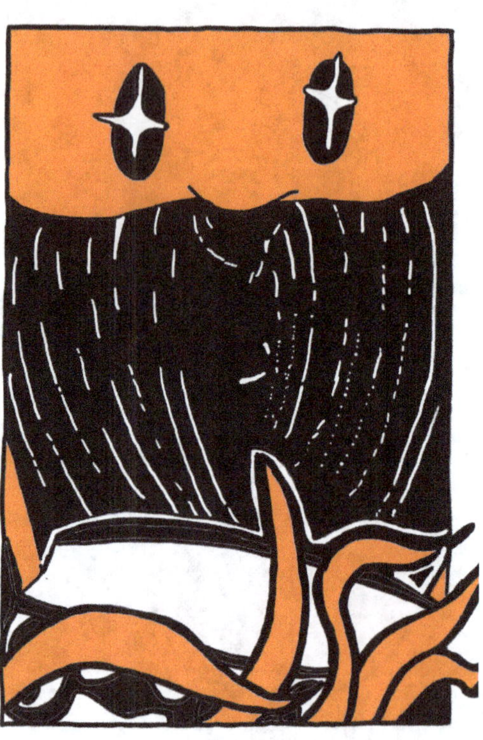
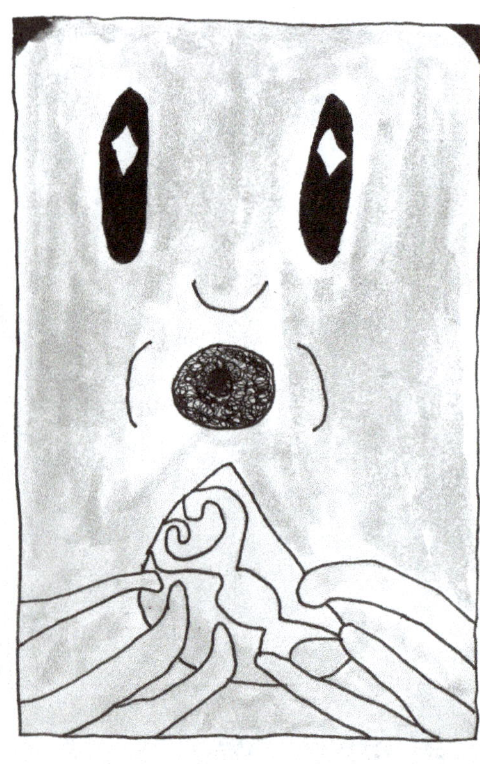
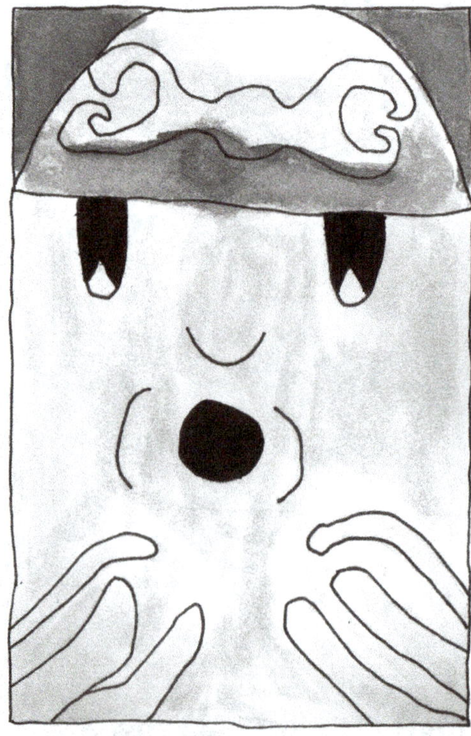
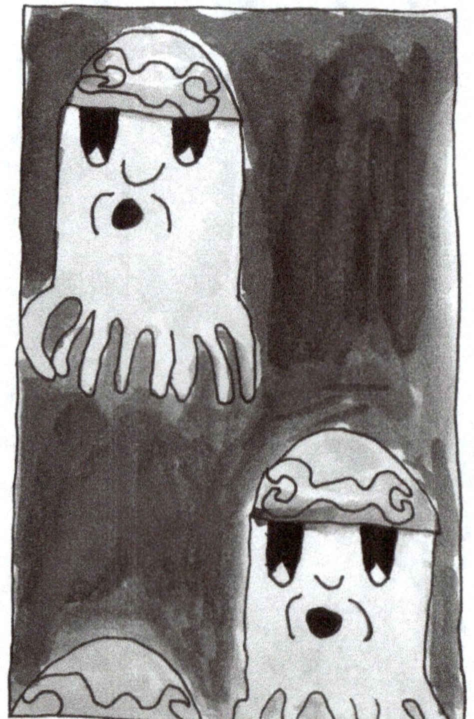

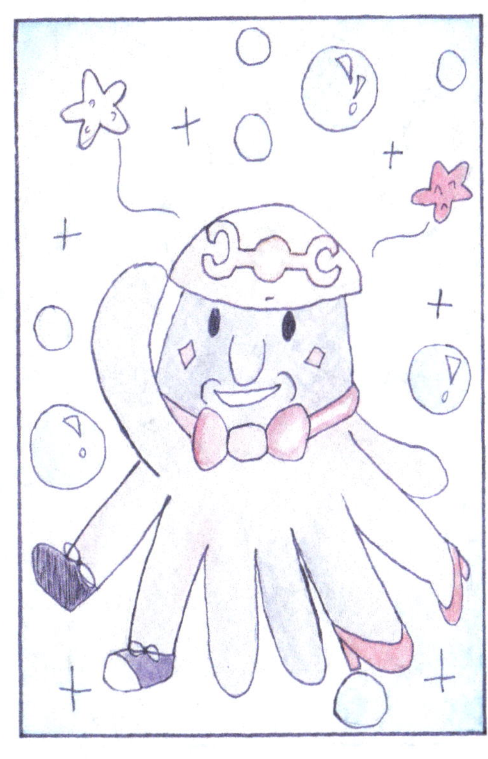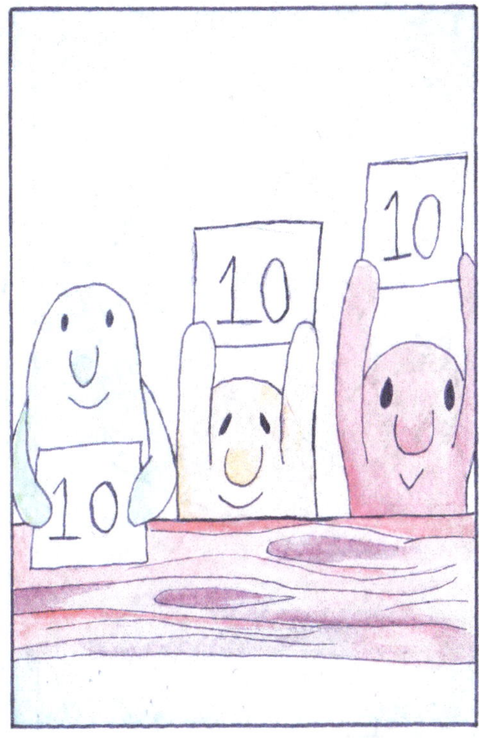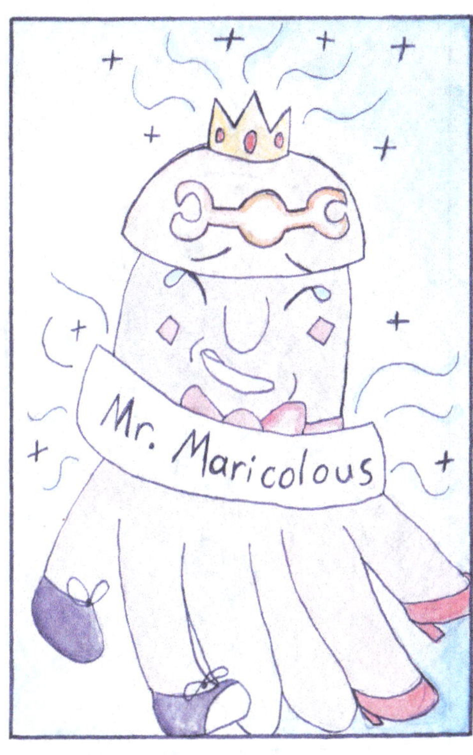

MARICOLOUS ZEGEINE CERAUNOGRAPH

Panels 1-3
Illustrator, Ink: Jennifer Pagan; Digital Color: Samantha Zarate

Panels 4-6
Illustrator, Ink: Devin Brown; and Ink Wash: Theodore Fuller

Panels 7-9
Illustrator: Spike Harris; Ink: Kiersten Kozlowski; Watercolor: Mason Higgins

MAYA'S SANDWiCHES

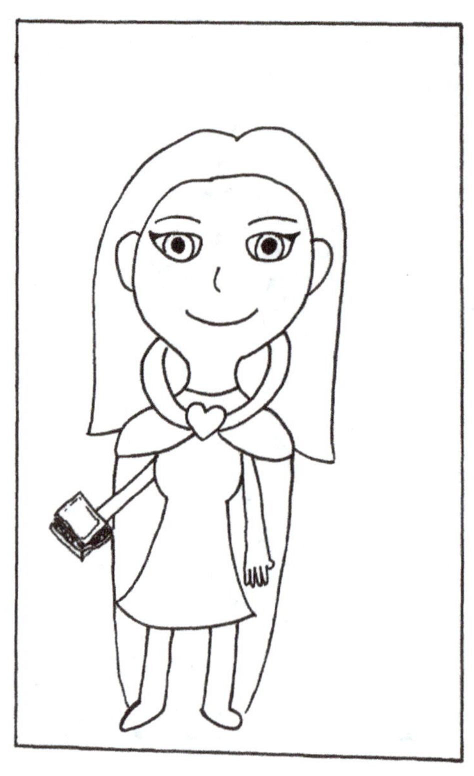

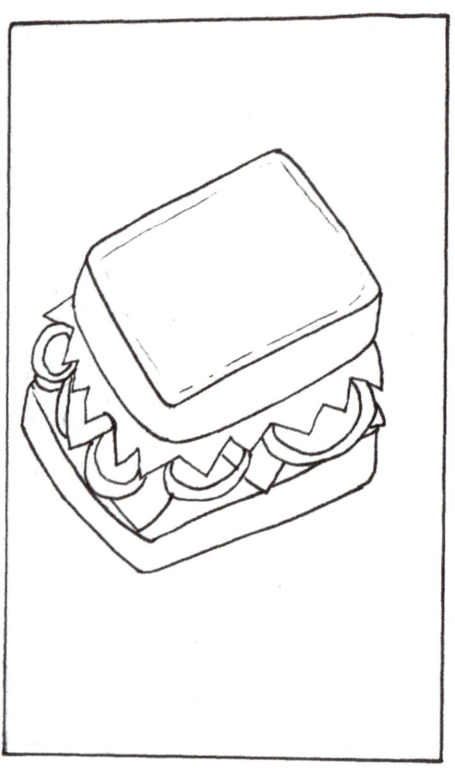

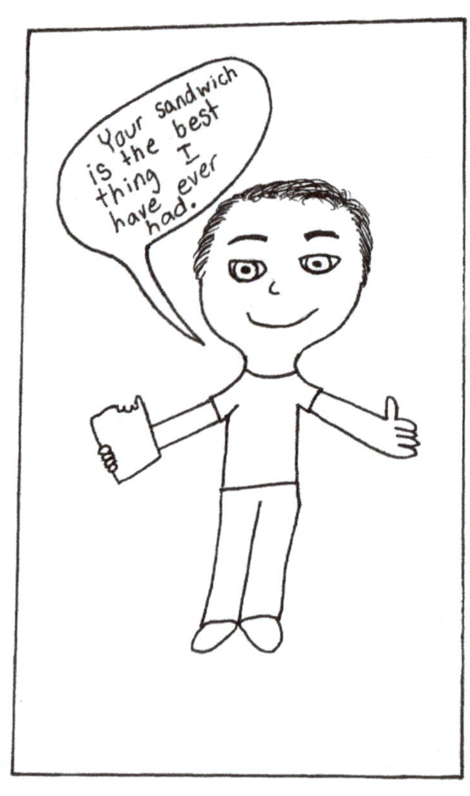

Your sandwich is the best thing I have ever had.

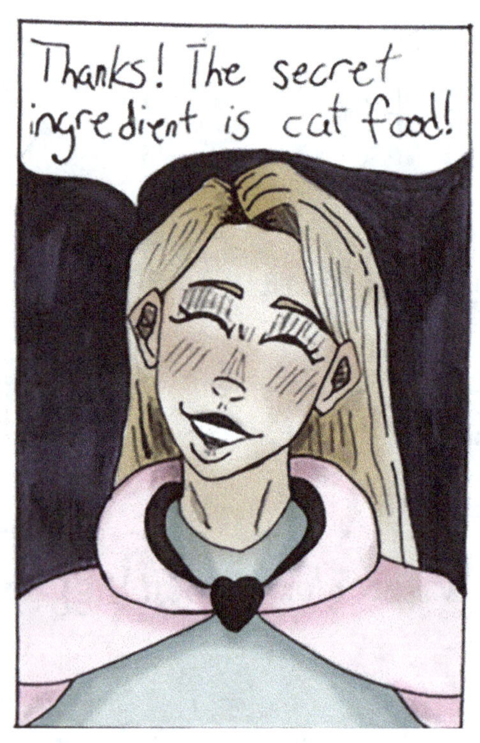

Thanks! The secret ingredient is cat food!

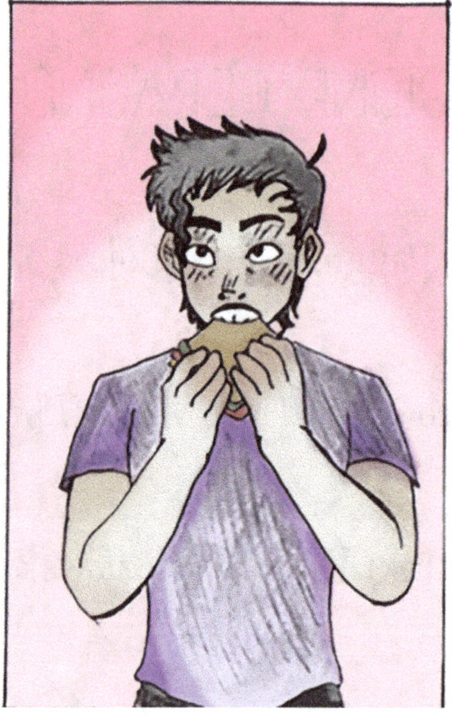

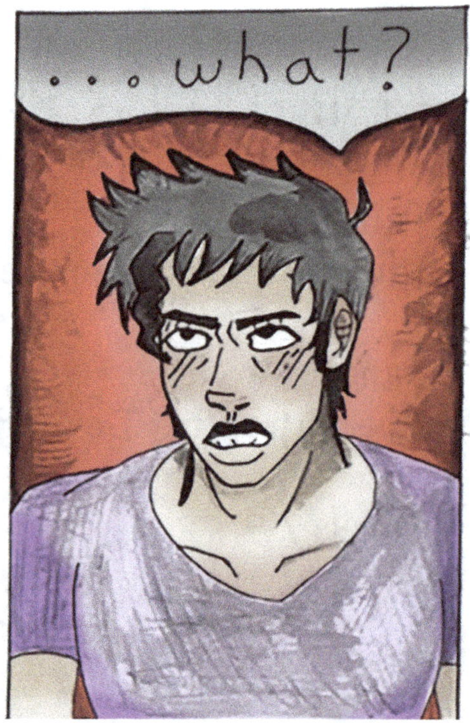

....what?

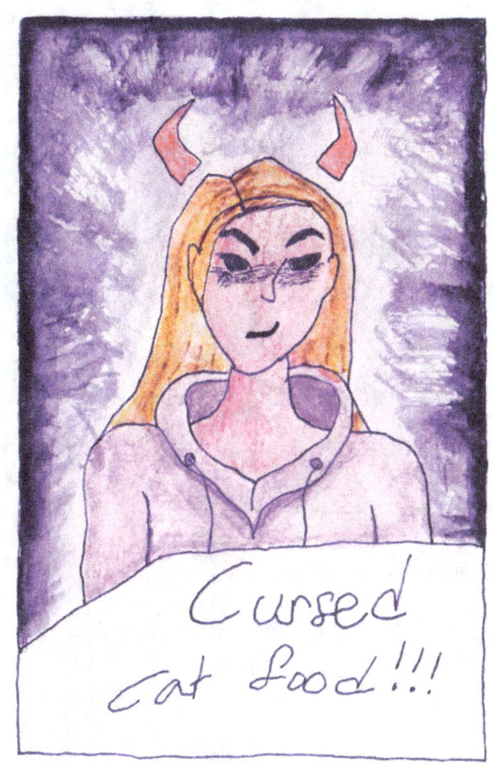

Cursed
cat food!!!

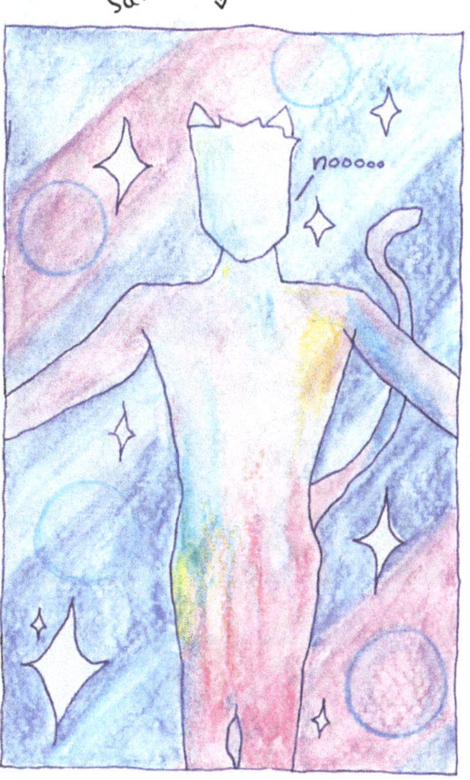

Sailor
noooo

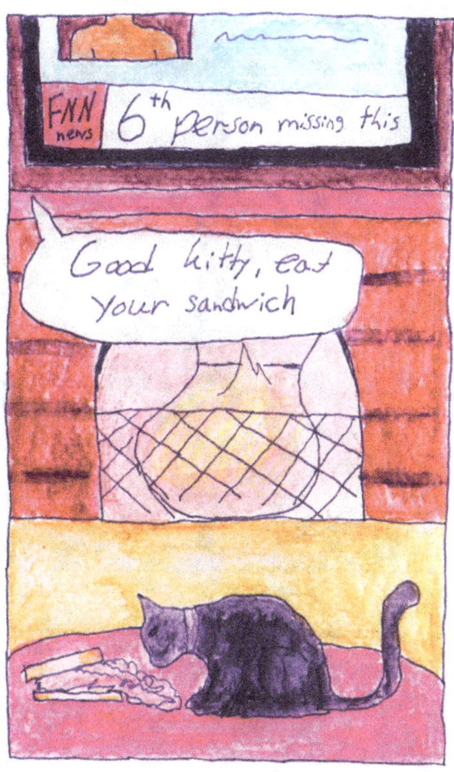

FNN news
6th person missing this
Good kitty, eat your sandwich

MAYA'S SANDWICHES

Panels 1-3
Illustrator: Tianne Murray; Ink: Dempsey Langan

Panels 4-6
Illustrator, Digital Color: Kiersten Kozlowski; Ink and Wash: Spike Harris

Panels 7-9
Illustrator, Ink: Ryan Ackerman; Watercolor: Spike Harris

MEAN GIRLS

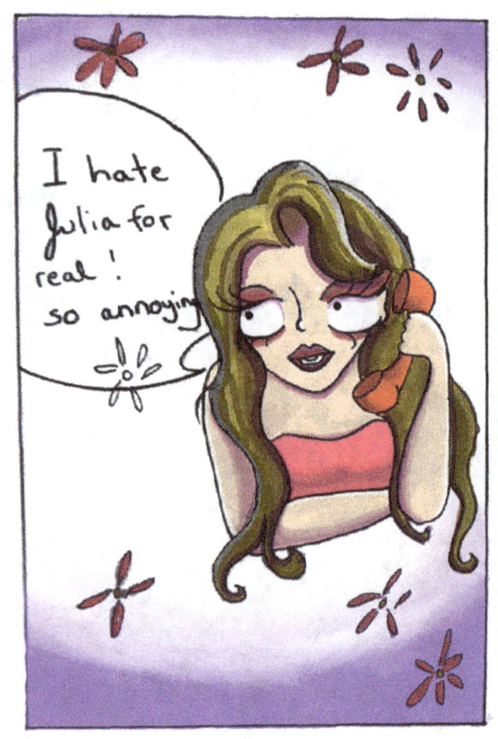

I hate Julia for real! so annoying

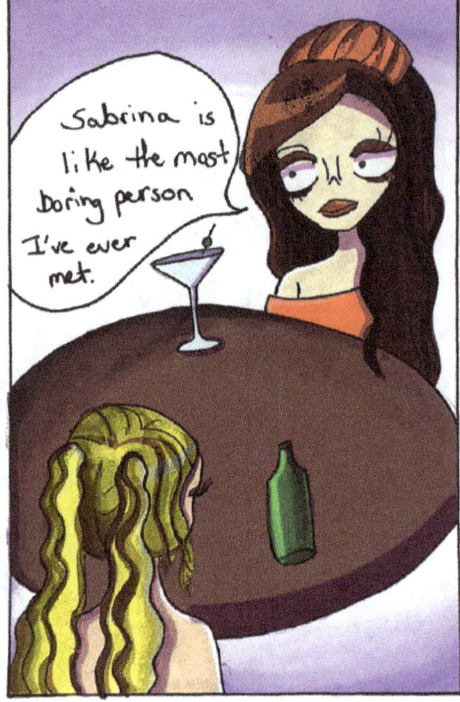

Sabrina is like the most boring person I've ever met.

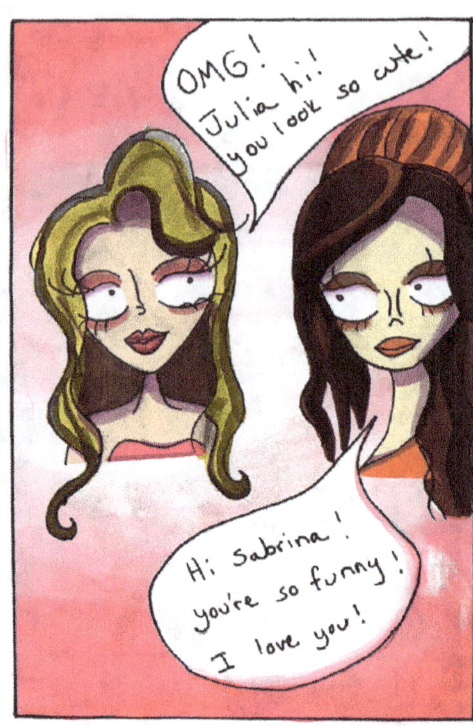

OMG! Julia hi! you look so cute!
Hi Sabrina! you're so funny! I love you!

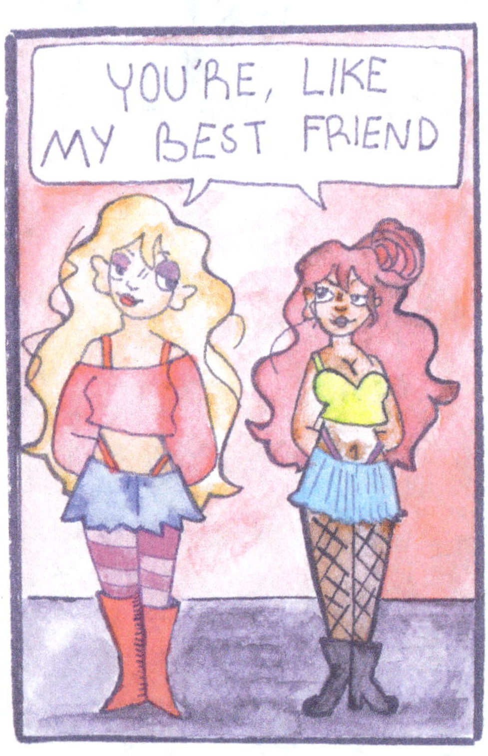

YOU'RE, LIKE MY BEST FRIEND

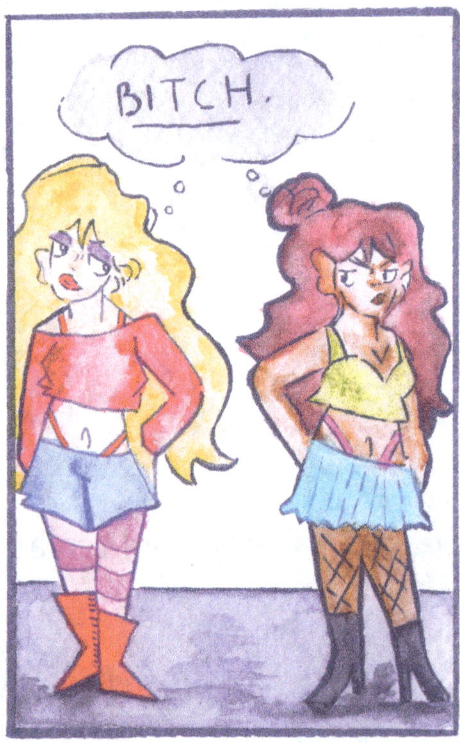

BITCH.

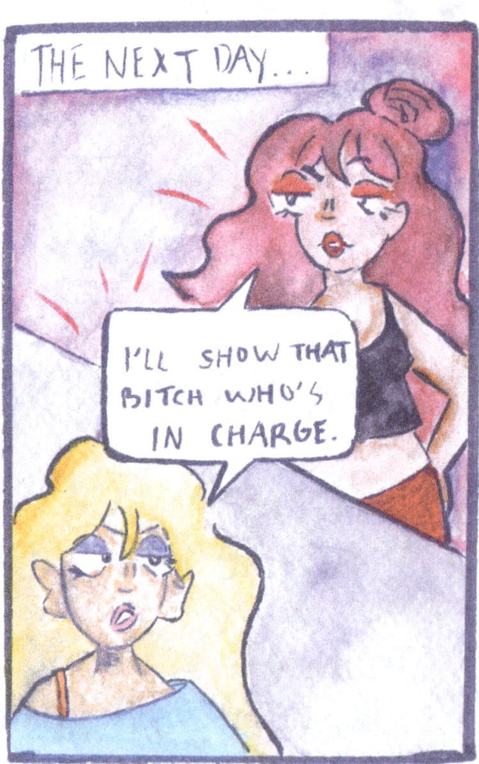

THE NEXT DAY...
I'LL SHOW THAT BITCH WHO'S IN CHARGE.

Panels 1-3
Illustrator: Mason Higgins; Ink and Wash: Kiersten Kozlowski;
Digital Color: Christopher Light

Panels 4-6
Illustrator: Casper Saez; , Ink: Christopher Light; Watercolor: Ayden Pigeon

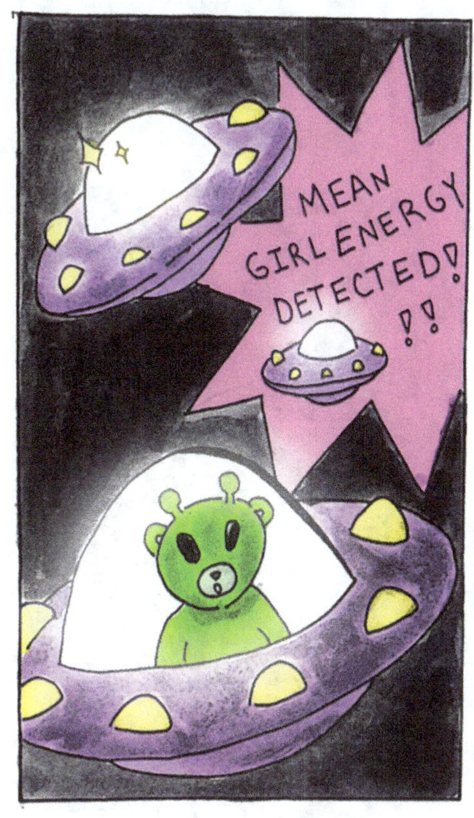

MEAN GIRL ENERGY DETECTED!!!

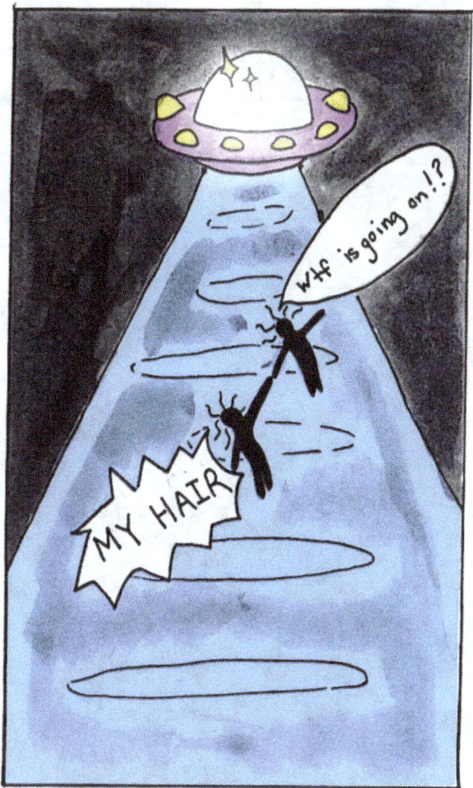

wtf is going on!?
MY HAIR

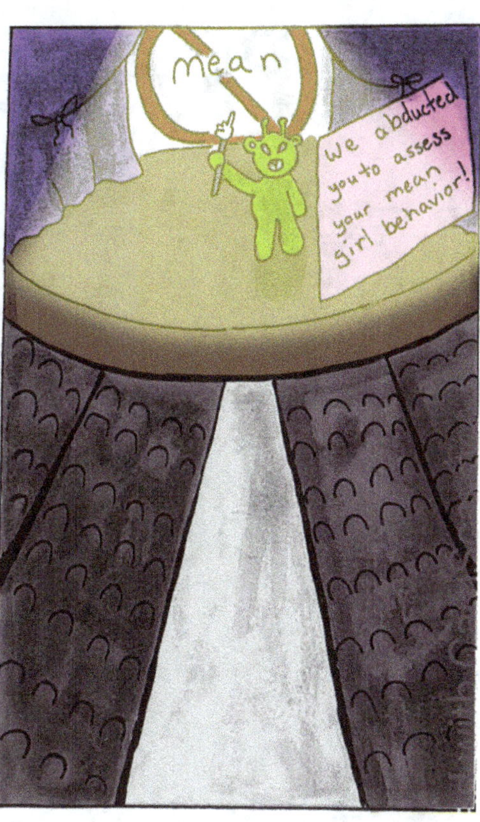

mean
We abducted you to assess your mean girl behavior!

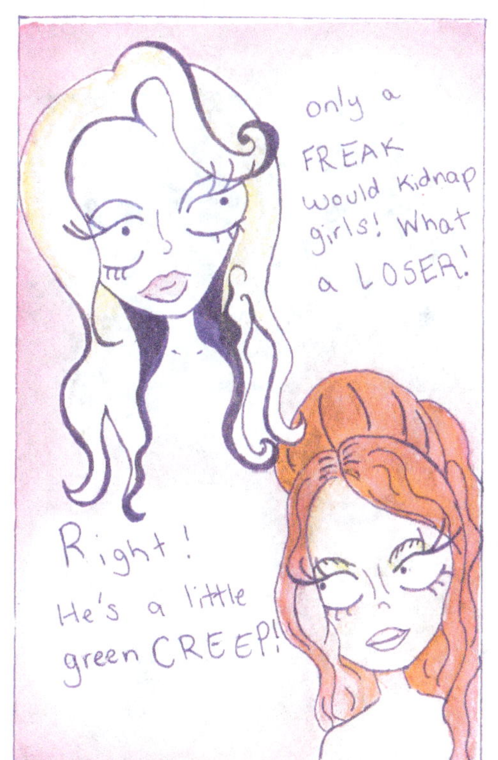

only a FREAK would kidnap girls! What a LOSER!
Right! He's a little green CREEP!

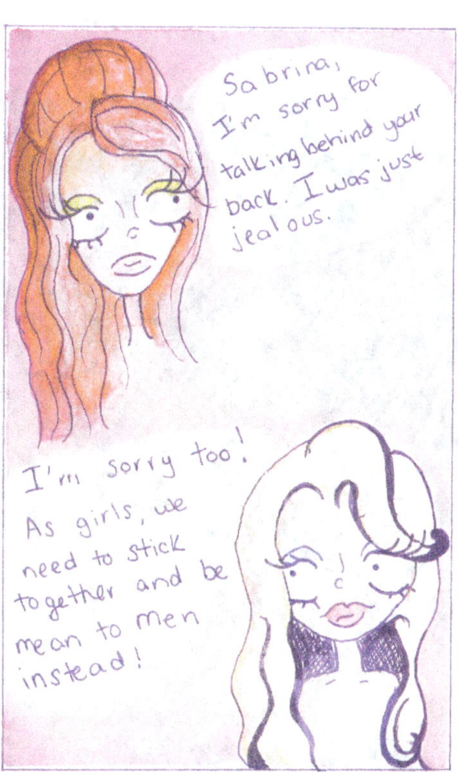

Sabrina, I'm sorry for talking behind your back. I was just jealous.
I'm sorry too! As girls, we need to stick together and be mean to men instead!

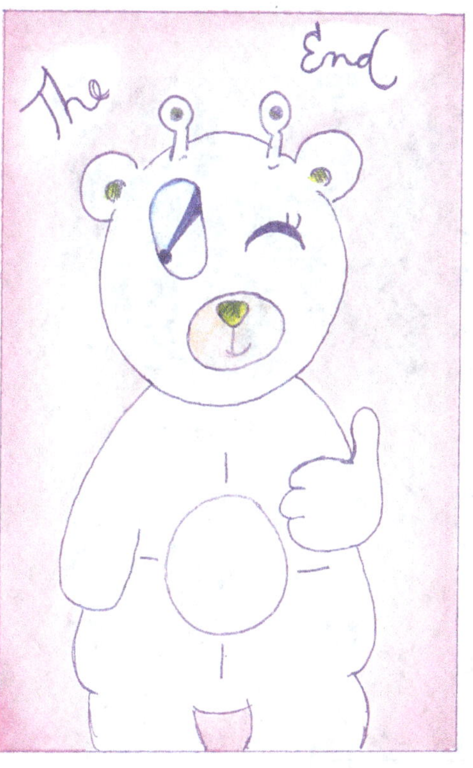

The End

Panels 7-9
Illustrator, Digital Color: Mason Higgins; Ink: Kalista Weed;
Ink Wash: Nicole Kolakowski;

Panels 10-12
Illustrator: Mason Higgins; Ink: Ayden Pigeon; Watercolor: Alina Jones

PEANUT BOMB ESCAPE

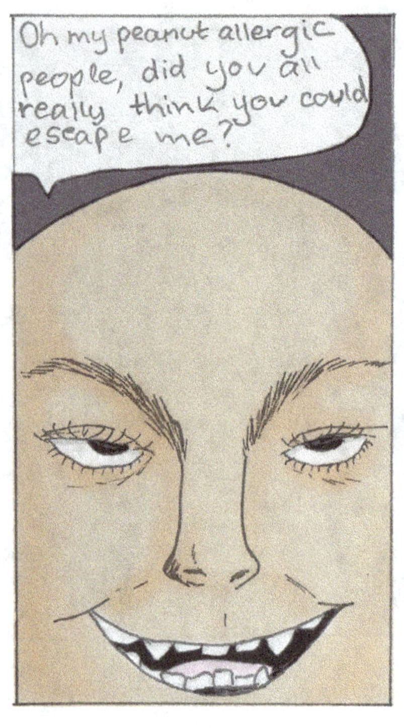

Oh my peanut allergic people, did you all really think you could escape me?

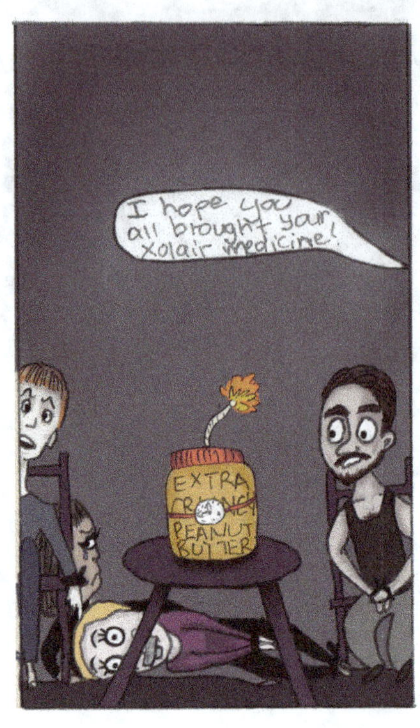

I hope you all brought your Xolair medicine!
EXTRA CRUNCHY PEANUT BUTTER

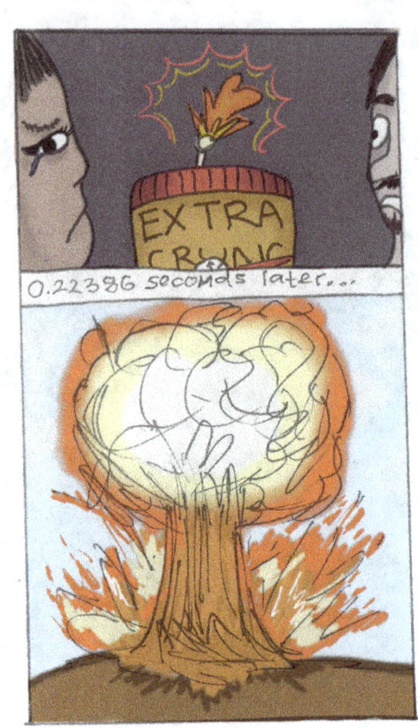

EXTRA CRUNC
0.22386 seconds later...

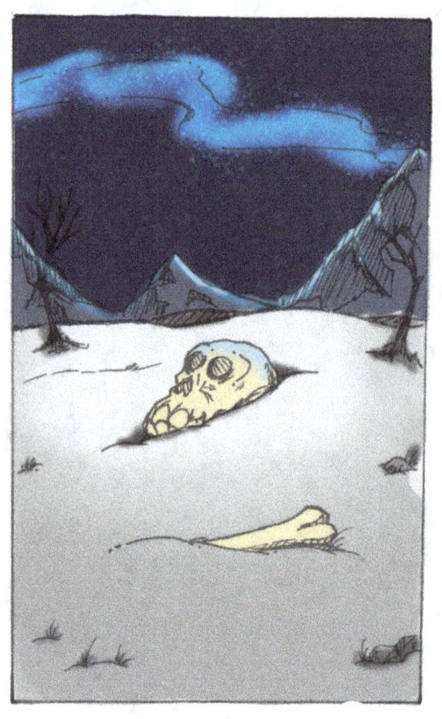

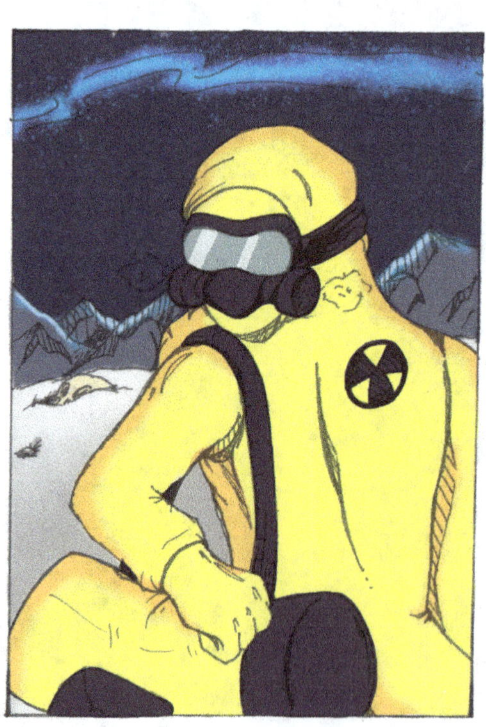

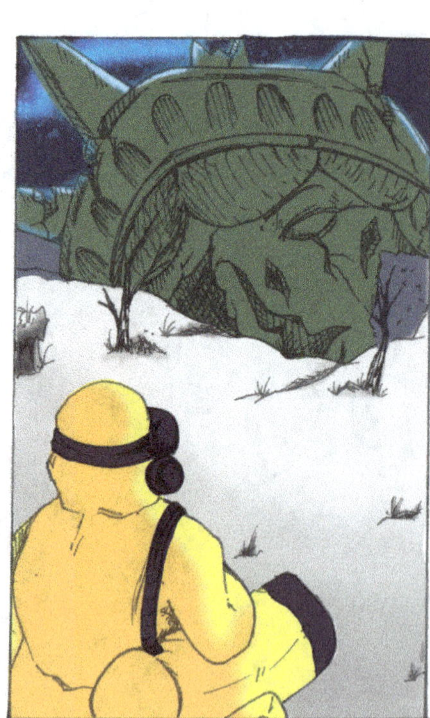

Panels 1-3
Illustrator: Megan Hardest; Ink: Leah Braverman; Digital Color: Mia Jones
Panels 4-6
Illustrator: Theodore Fuller; Ink and Digital Color: Alina Jones

SAUSAGE MAP EXPLODE

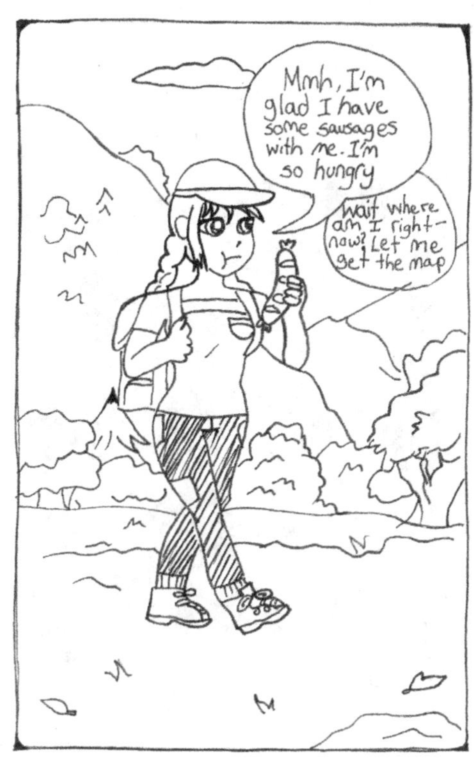

Mmh, I'm glad I have some sausages with me. I'm so hungry
Wait where am I right now? Let me get the map

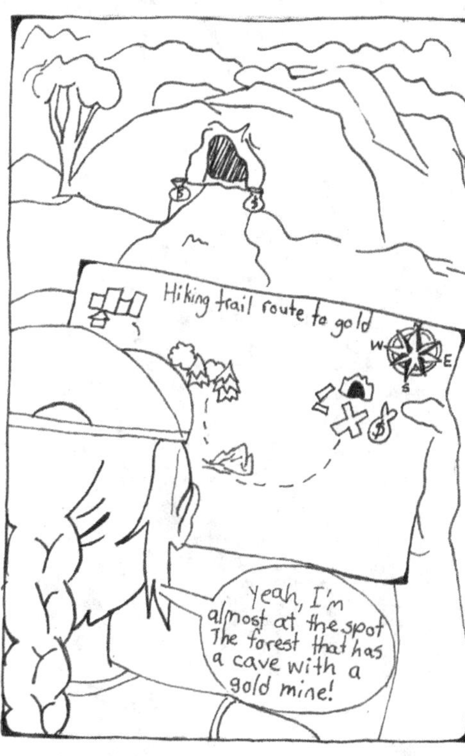

Hiking trail route to gold
W N E S
Yeah, I'm almost at the spot The forest that has a cave with a gold mine!

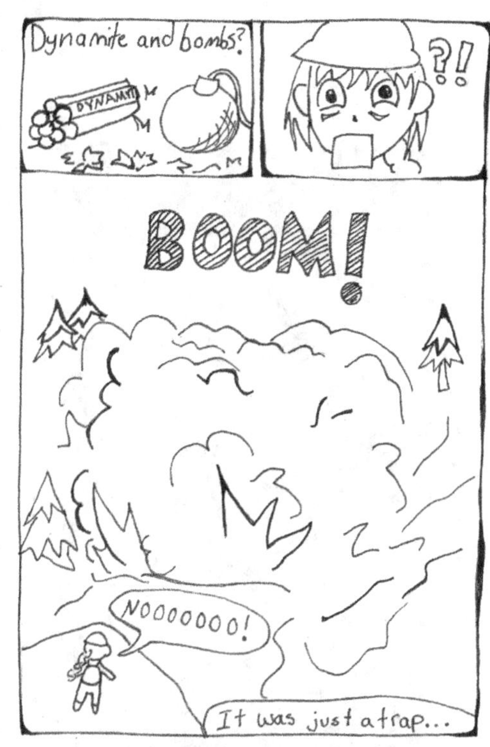

Dynamite and bombs?
DYNAMITE
?!
BOOM!
NOOOOOOO!
It was just a trap...

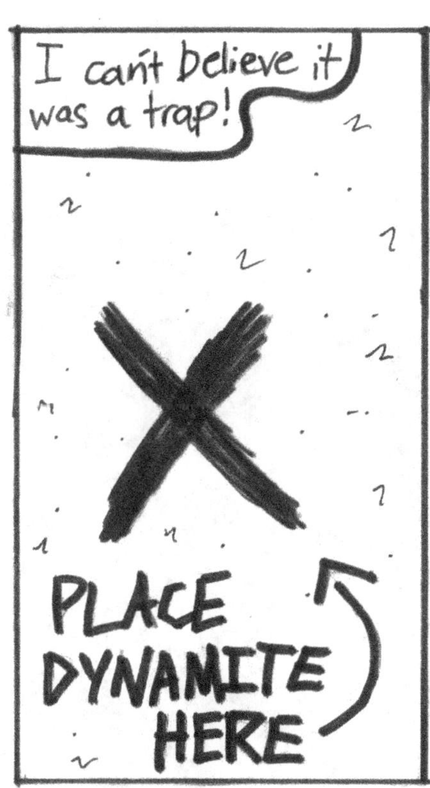

I can't believe it was a trap!
PLACE DYNAMITE HERE

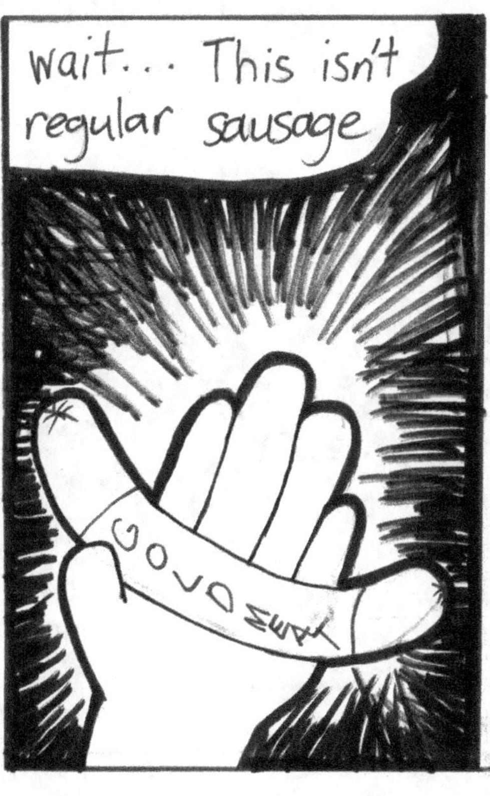

Wait... This isn't regular sausage
GOLD SAUSAGE

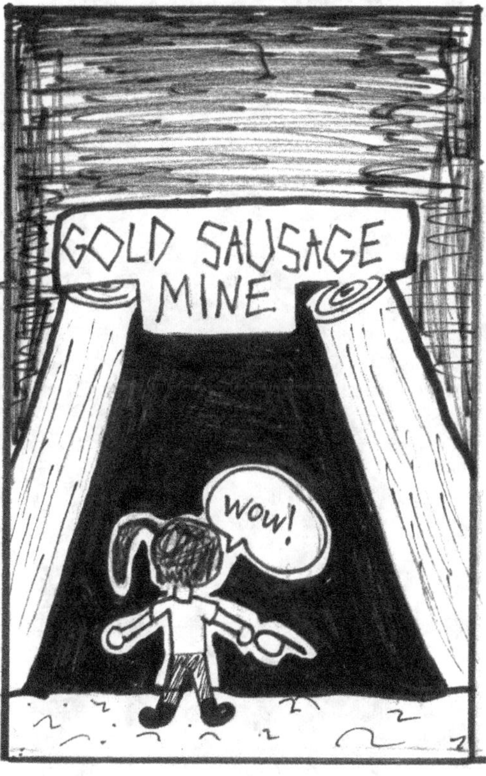

GOLD SAUSAGE MINE
WOW!

Panels 1-3
Illustrator: Nicole Kolakowski; Ink: Mason Higgins
Panels 4-6
Illustrator: Devin Brown; Ink: Spike Harris

SHADOW CREATURE FEDERATION

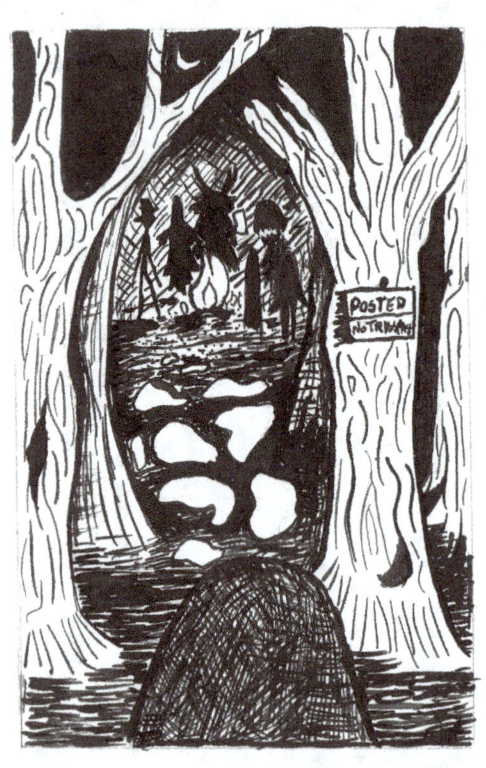

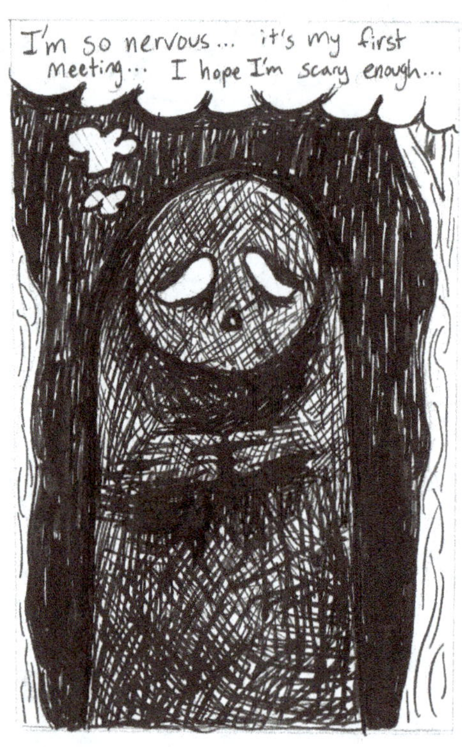

I'm so nervous... it's my first meeting... I hope I'm scary enough...

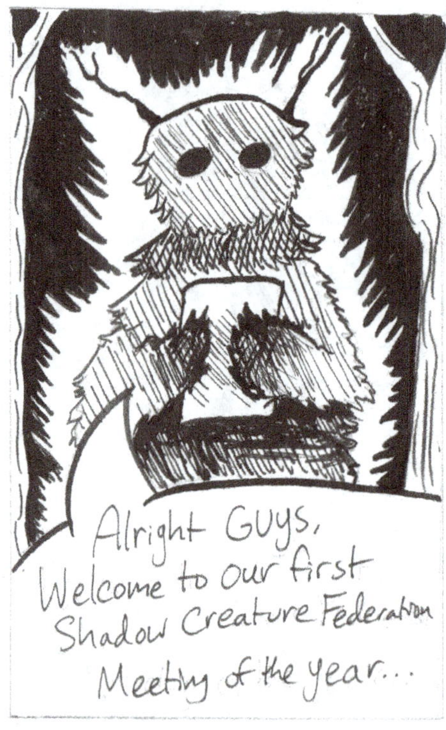

Alright Guys, Welcome to our first Shadow Creature Federation Meeting of the year...

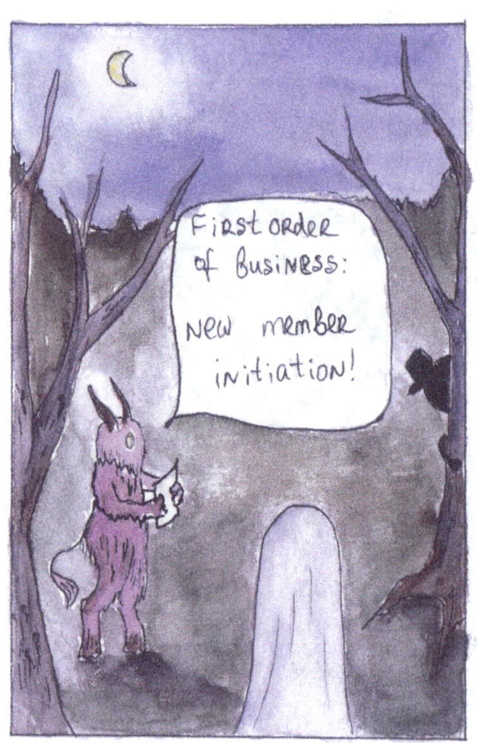

First order of business: New member initiation!

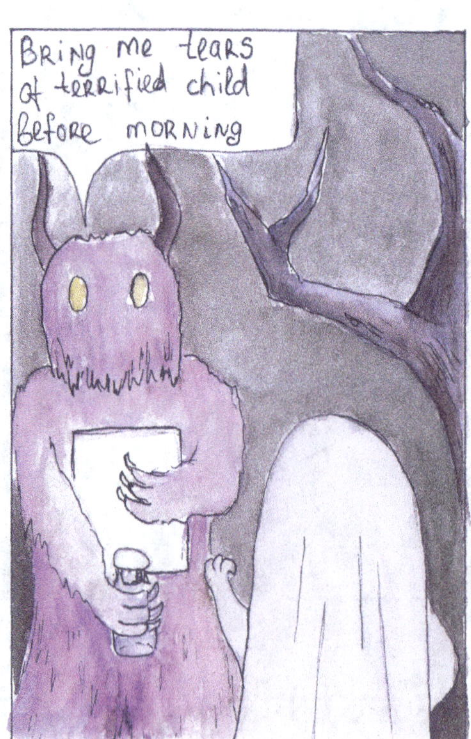

Bring me tears of terrified child Before MORNING

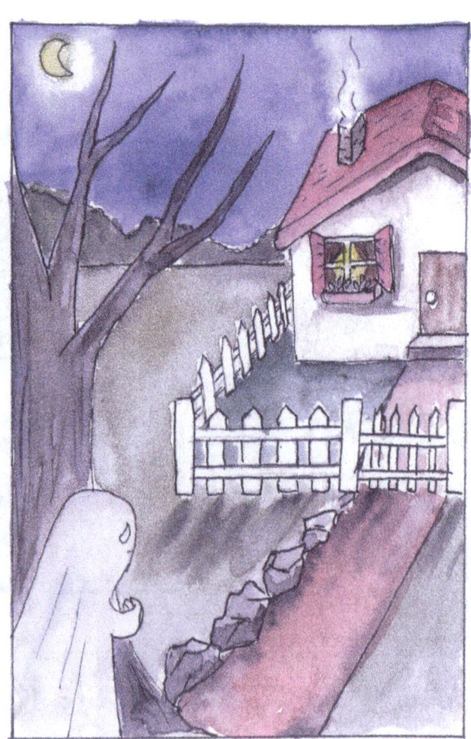

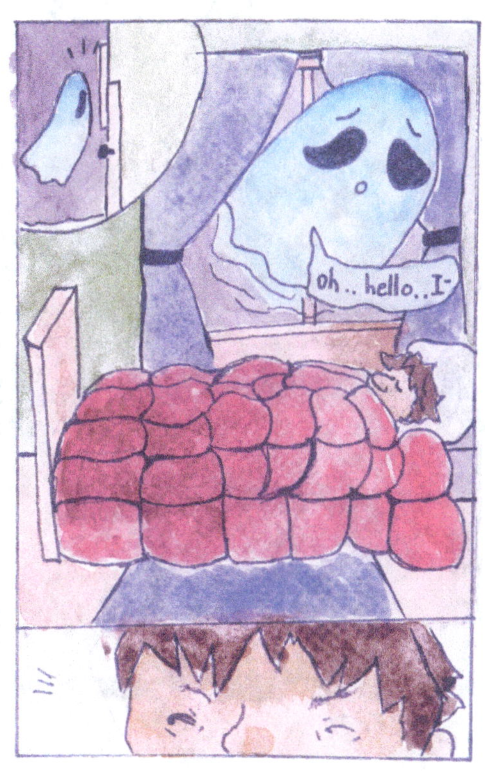

oh..hello..I-

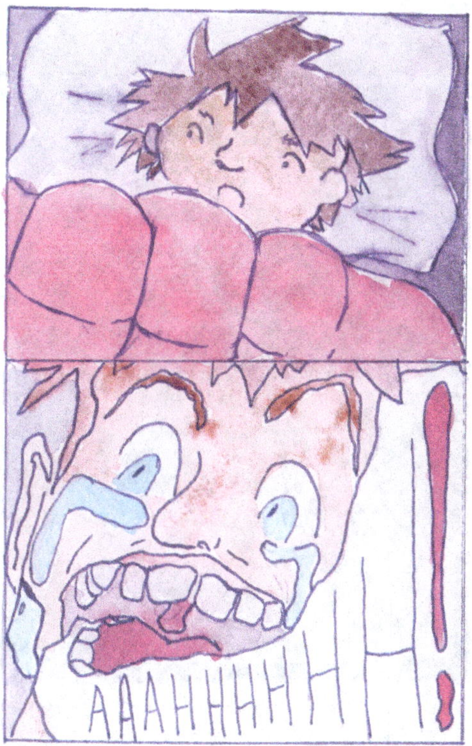

AAAHHHHH

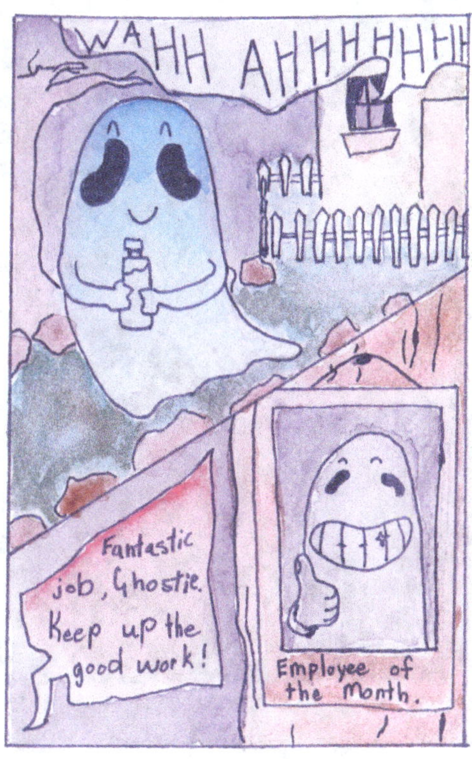

WAHH AHHHHHHH
Fantastic job, Ghostie. Keep up the good work!
Employee of the Month.

SHADOW CREATURE FEDERATION

Panels 1-3
Illustrator, Ink: Mia Jones

Panels 4-6
Illustrator, Ink, and Water Color: Leah Braverman

Panels 7-9
Illustrator: Kalista Weed; Ink and Water Color: Ryan Ackerman

Smelly Feather Polish

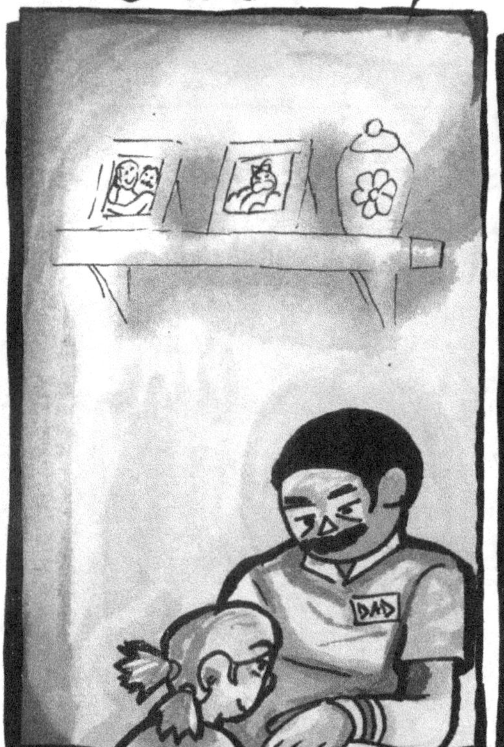

DAD

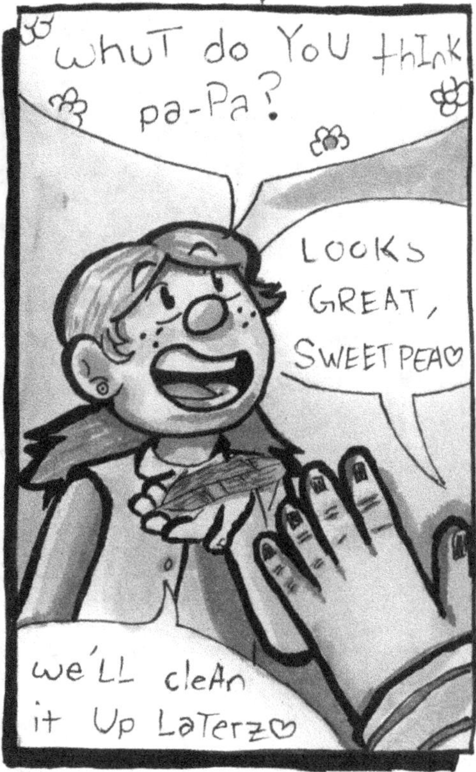

WHUT do YOU thInk pa-Pa?
LOOKS GREAT, SWEETPEA♡
we'LL cleAn it Up Laterz♡

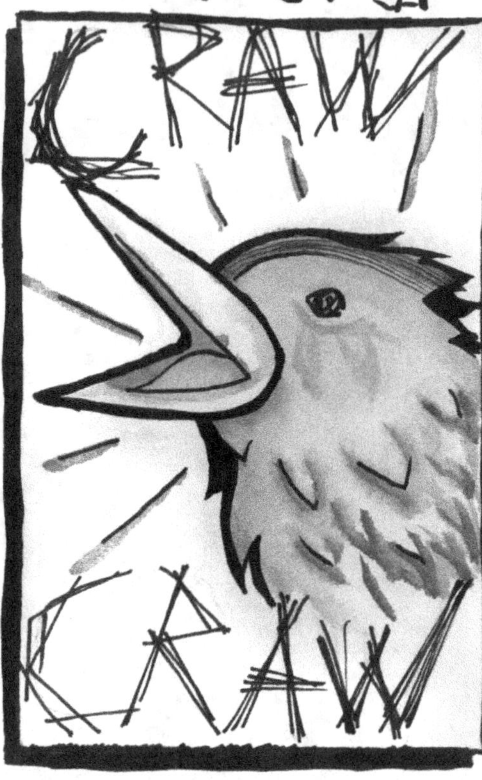

CRAW
KRAW

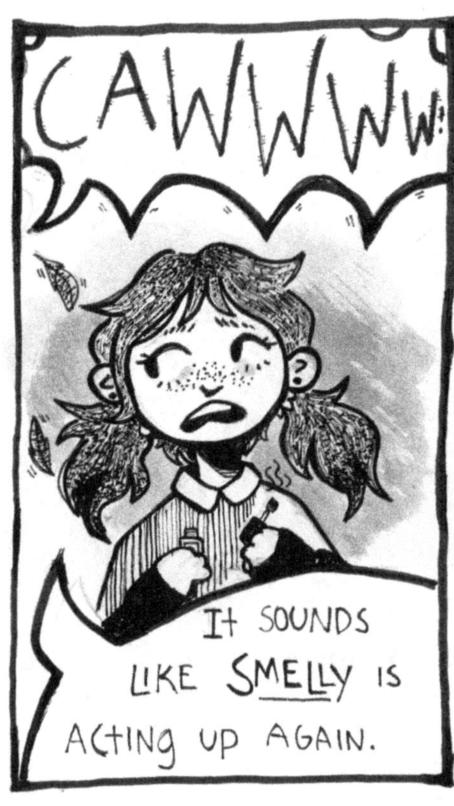

CAWWWW!
It SOUNDS LIKE SMELLY IS ACTING UP AGAIN.

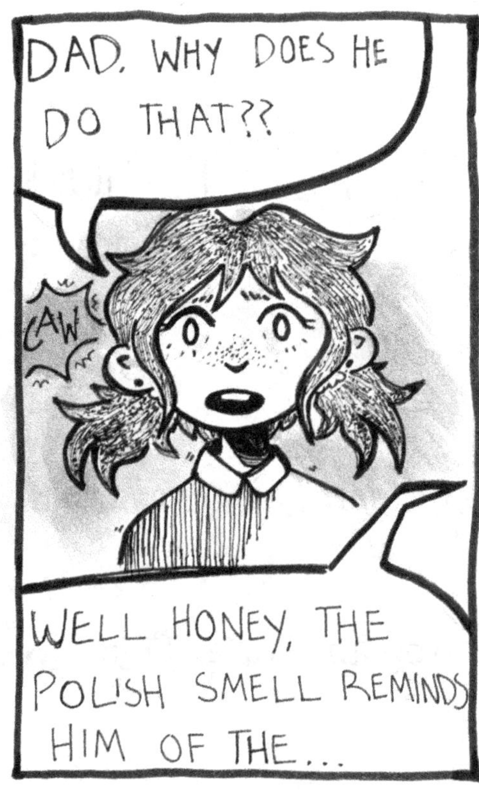

DAD. WHY DOES HE DO THAT??
CAW
WELL HONEY, THE POLISH SMELL REMINDS HIM OF THE...

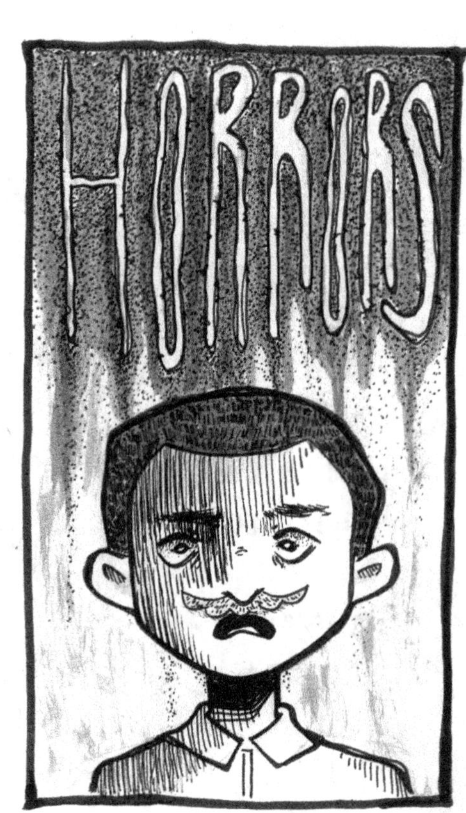

HORRORS

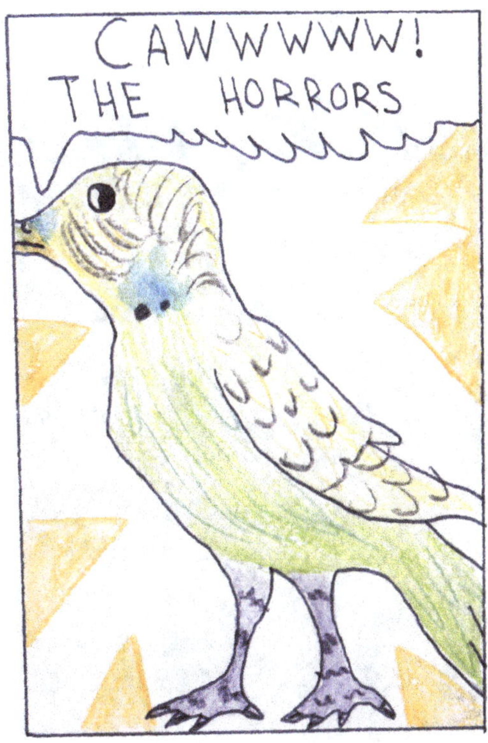

CAWWWWW! THE HORRORS

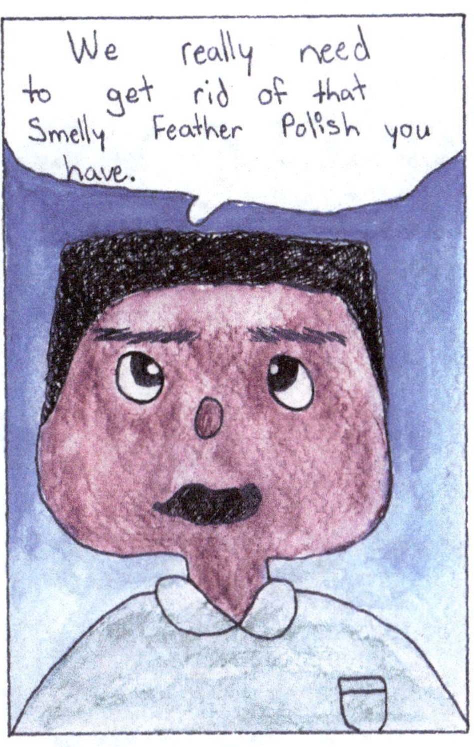

We really need to get rid of that Smelly Feather Polish you have.

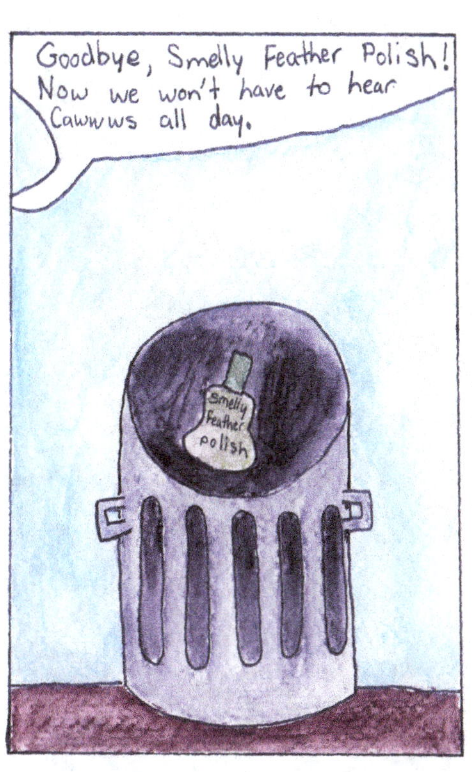

Goodbye, Smelly Feather Polish! Now we won't have to hear Cawwws all day.
Smelly Feather Polish

SMELLY FEATHER POLISH

Panels 1-3
Illustrator, Ink, and Color: Spike Harris; Digital: Christopher Light

Panels 4-6
Illustrator, Ink, and Ink Wash: Emily Brier

Panels 7-9
Illustrator: Mia Jones; Ink: Kiersten Kozlowski; Water Color: Kalista Weed

STANDARD BATTLE SAFETY

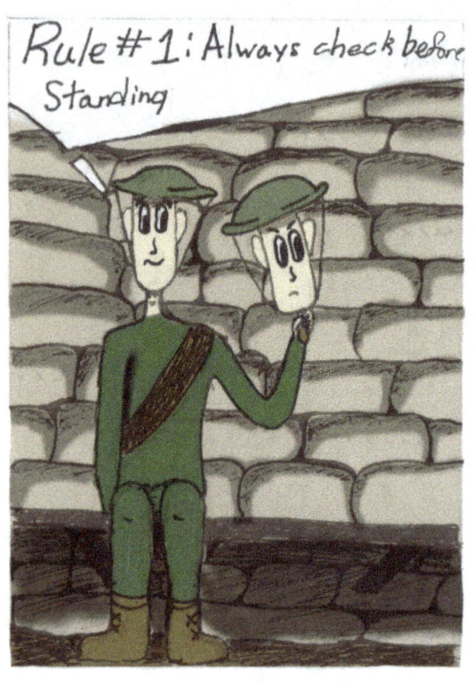

Rule #1: Always check before Standing

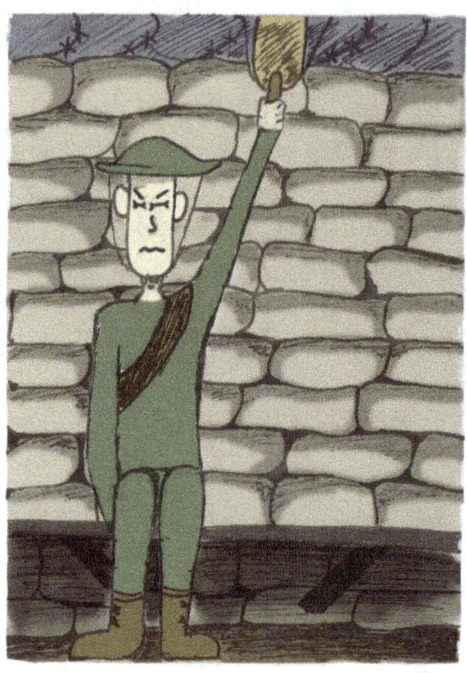

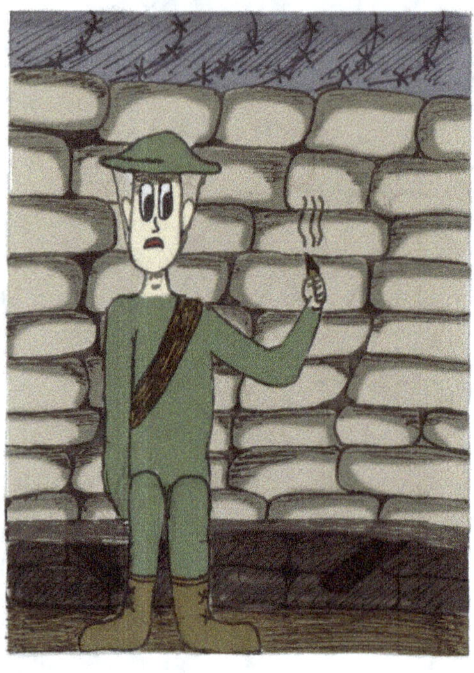

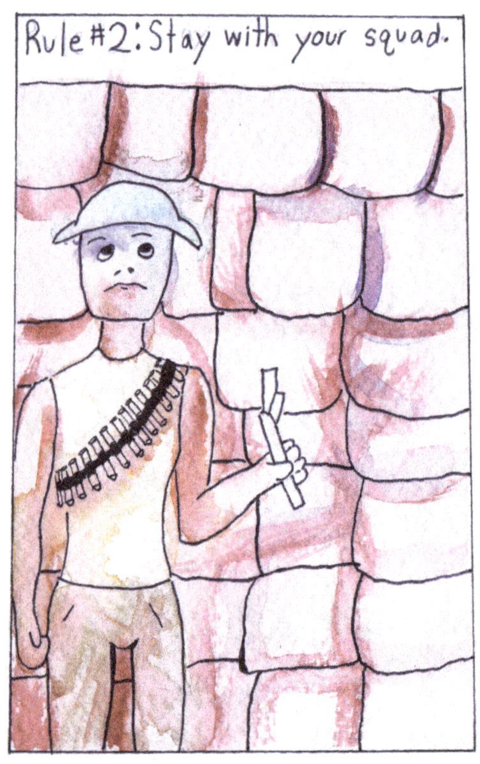

Rule #2: Stay with your squad.

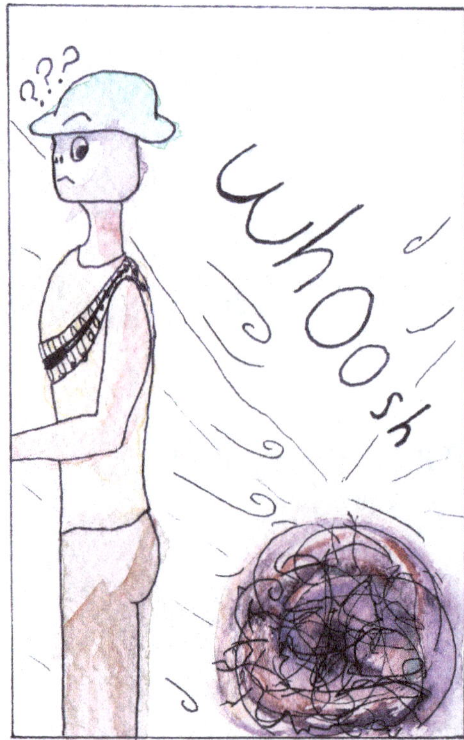

???
whoosh

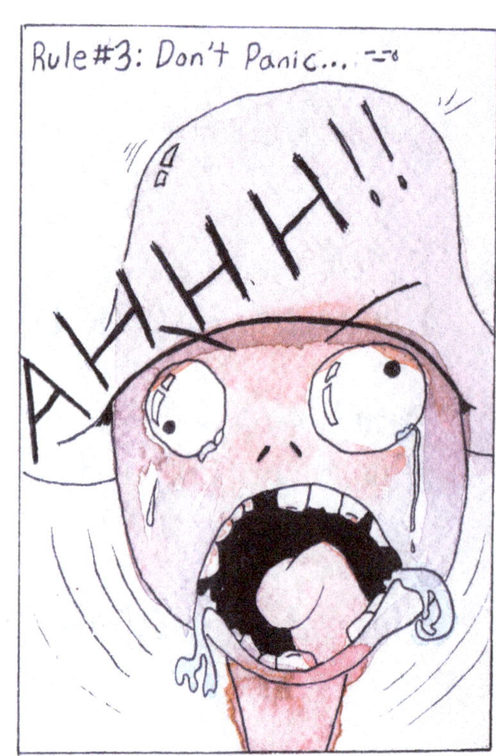

Rule #3: Don't Panic...
AHHH!!!

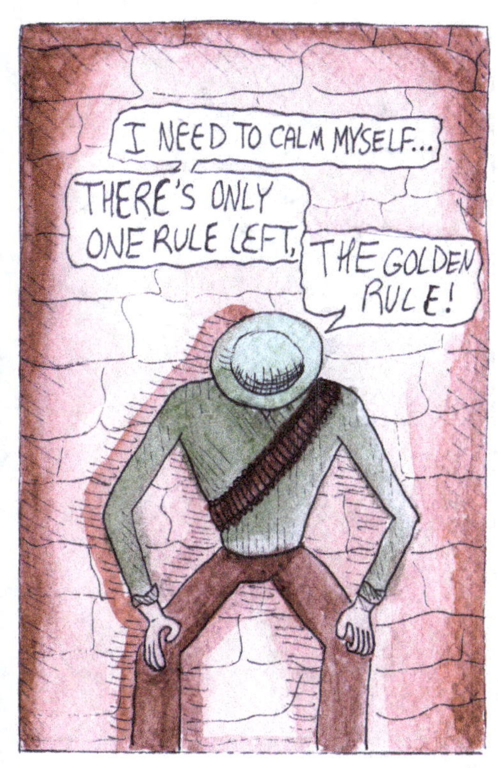

I NEED TO CALM MYSELF...
THERE'S ONLY ONE RULE LEFT,
THE GOLDEN RULE!

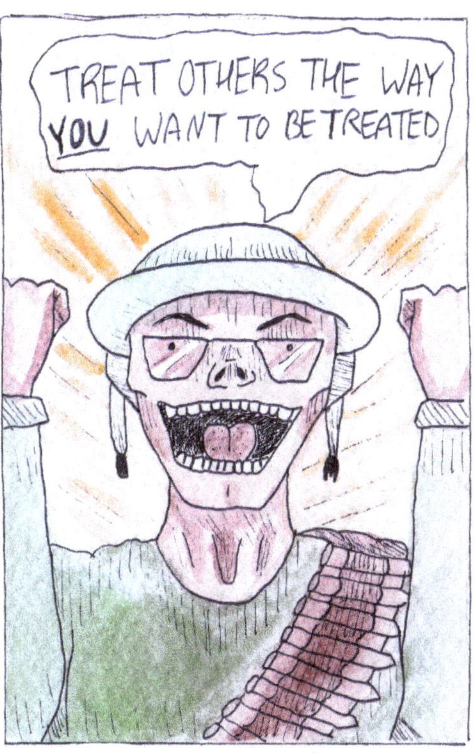

TREAT OTHERS THE WAY YOU WANT TO BE TREATED

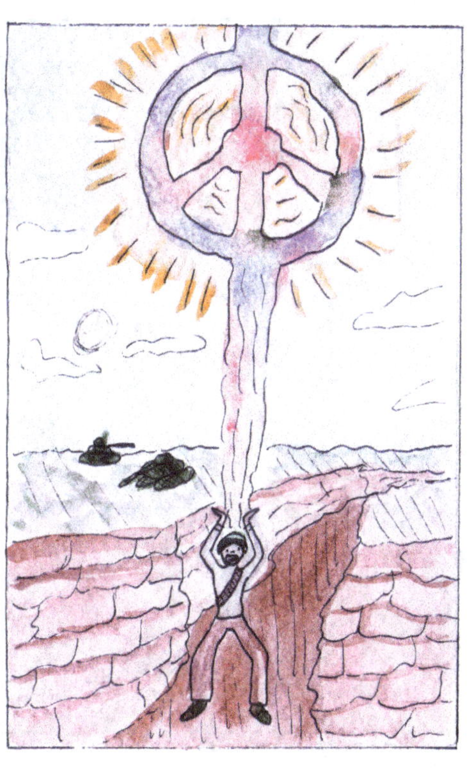

STANDARD BATTLE SAFETY

Panels 1-3
Illustrator, Ink, Digital Color: Ryan Ackerman

Panels 4-6
Illustrator and Watercolor: Jennifer Pagan; Ink: Dempsey Langan

Panels 7-9
Illustrator: Dempsey Langan; Ink and Watercolor: Mia Jones

THE FOX AND THE WOLF

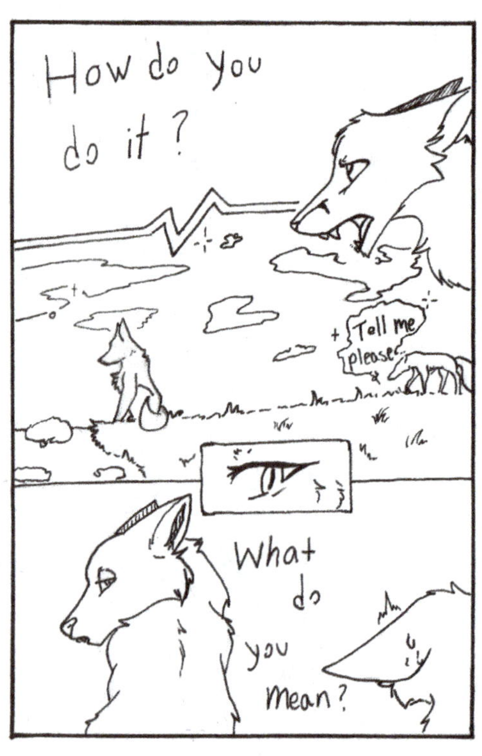

How do you do it?
+ Tell me please!
What do you mean?

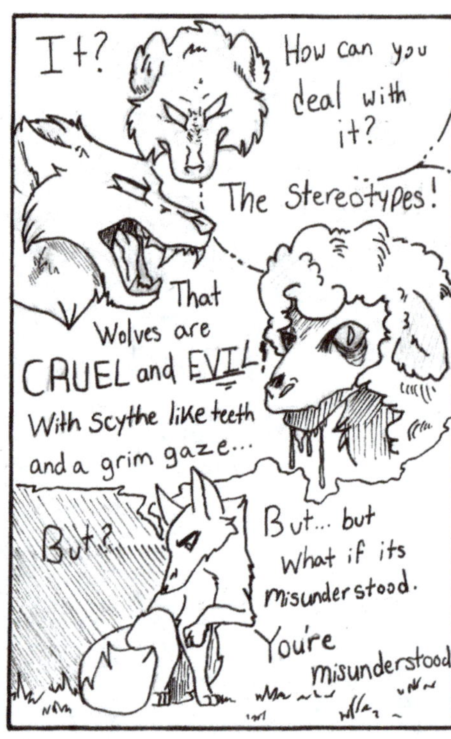

It? How can you deal with it?
The Stereotypes!
That Wolves are CRUEL and EVIL! With scythe like teeth and a grim gaze...
But?
But... but what if its misunderstood.
You're misunderstood

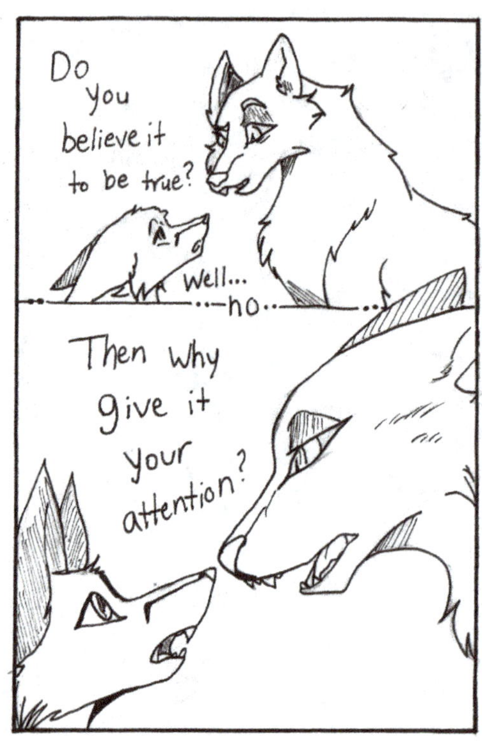

Do you believe it to be true?
Well... ...no...
Then why give it your attention?

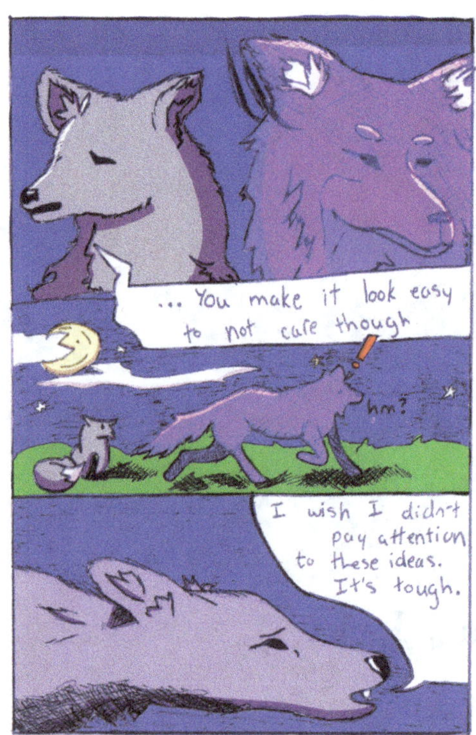

... You make it look easy to not care though
hm?
I wish I didn't pay attention to these ideas. It's tough.

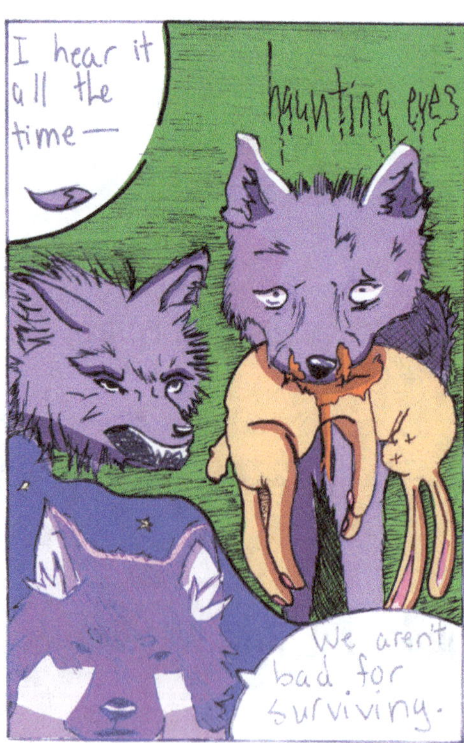

I hear it all the time —
haunting eyes
We aren't bad for surviving.

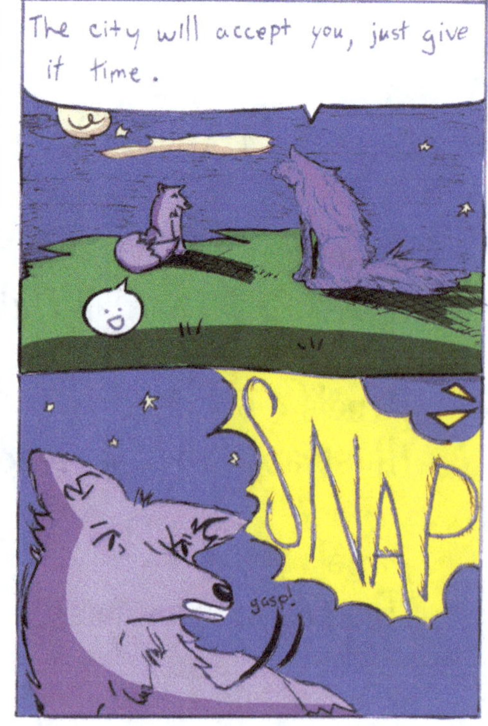

The city will accept you, just give it time.
SNAP
gasp.

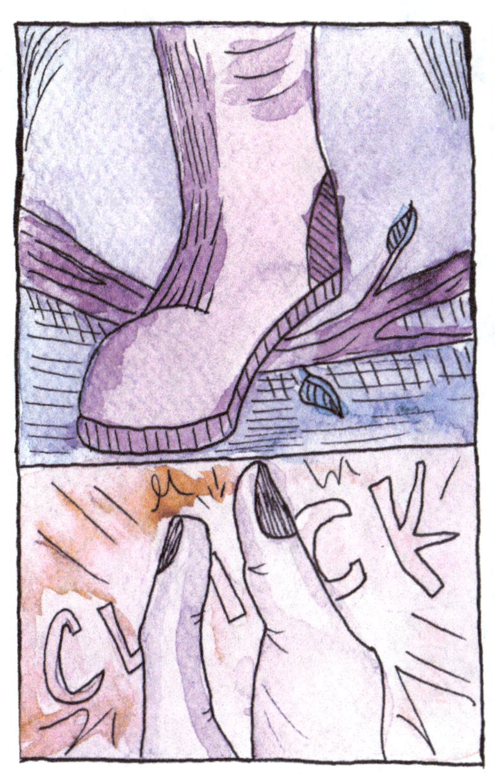

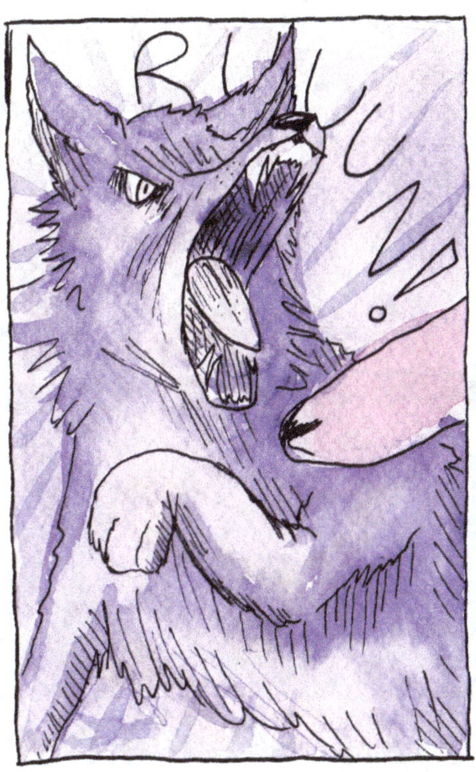

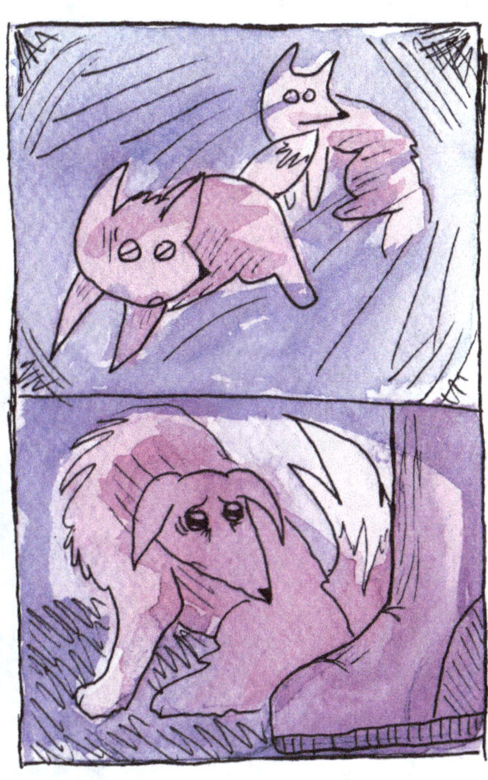

THE FOX AND THE WOLF

Panels 1-3
Illustrator: Alina Jones; Ink: Kalista Weed

Panels 4-6
Illustrator: Kalista Weed; Ink: Jennifer Pagan; Digital Color, Christopher Light

Panels 7-9
Illustrator: Theodore Fuller; Ink and Water Color: Mia Jones

THE PERFECT PRODUCT

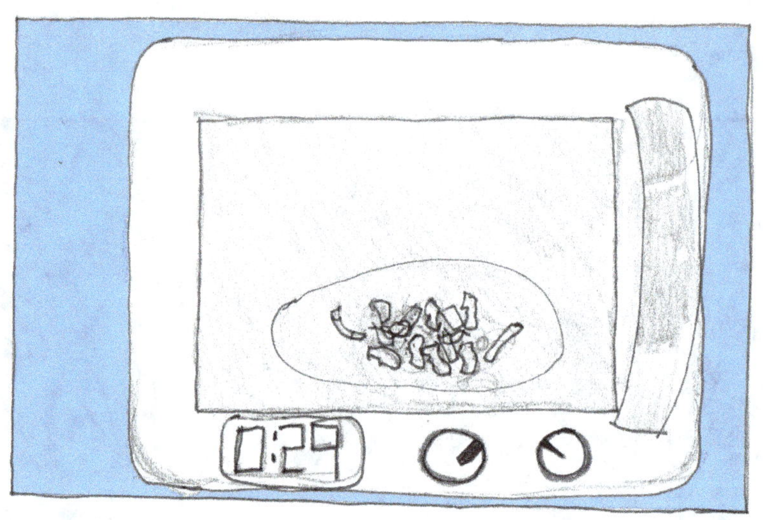

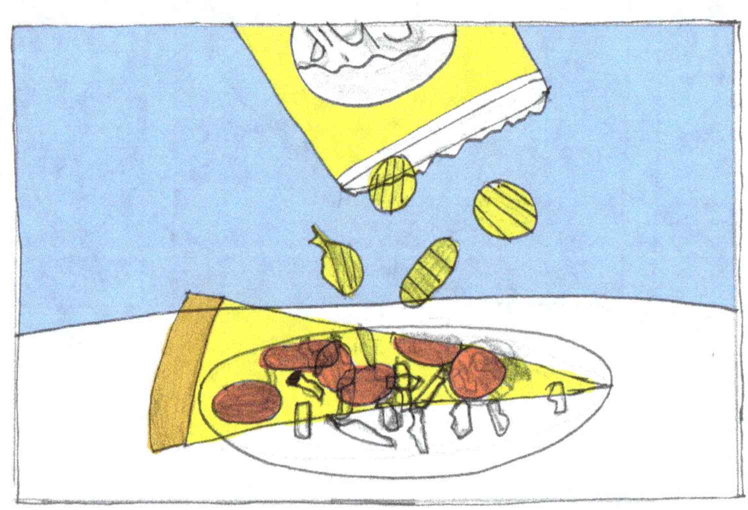

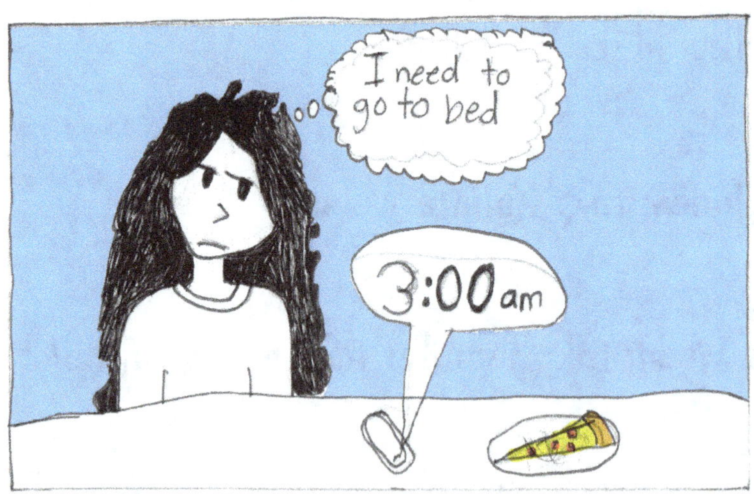

I need to
go to bed
3:00 am

Panels 1-3
Illustrator: Samantha Zarate; Ink and digital color: Tianne Murray

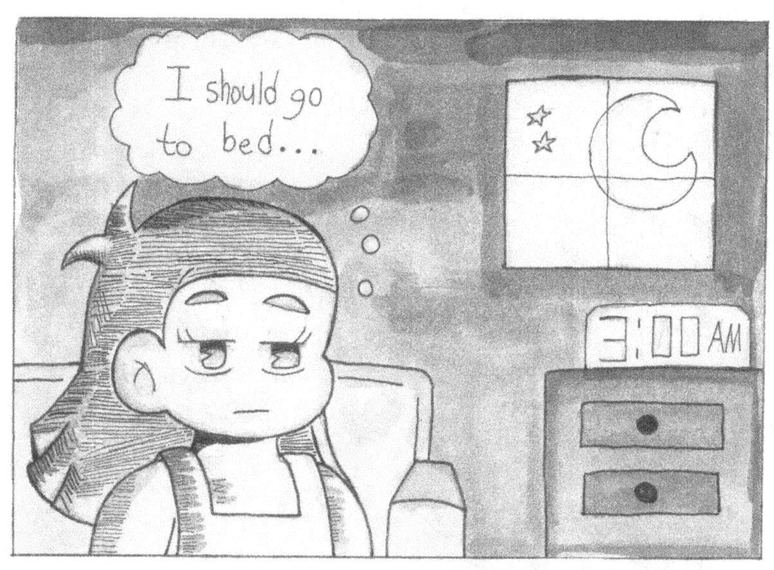

I should go to bed...
3:00 AM

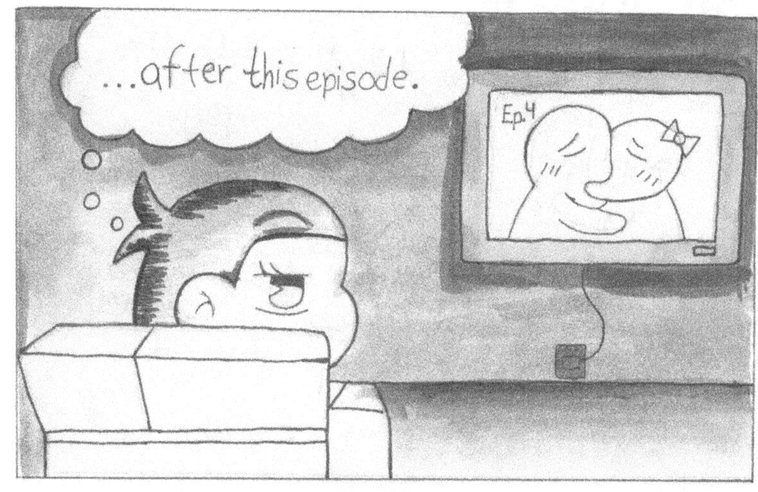

...after this episode.
Ep.4

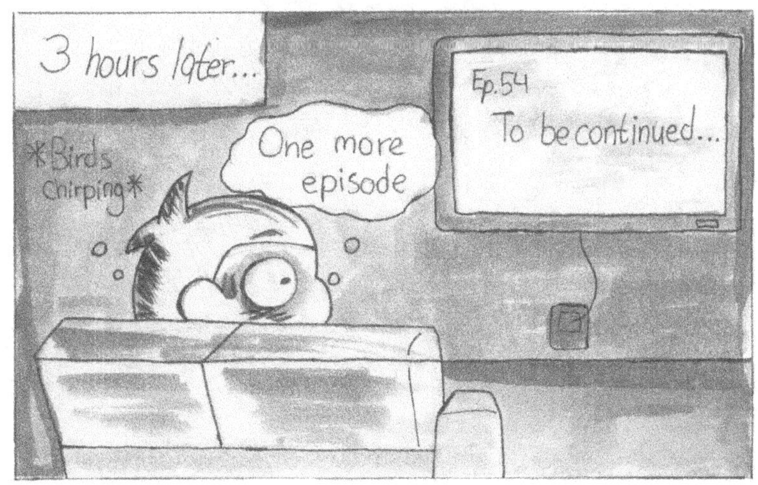

3 hours later...
Birds chirping
One more episode
Ep.54
To be continued...

Panels 4-6
Illustrator: Christopher Light; Ink: Nicole Kolakowski; Ink Wash: Ayden Pigeon

THE PERFECT PRODUCT, CONT'D

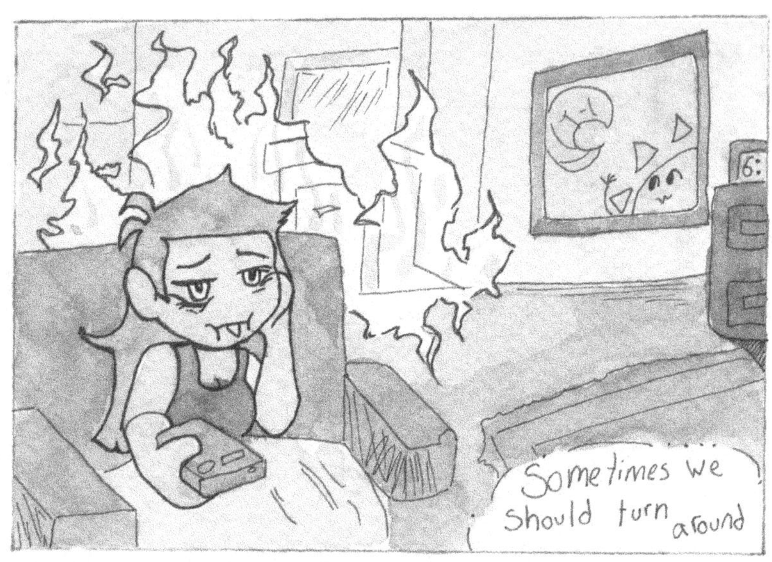

Sometimes we should turn around

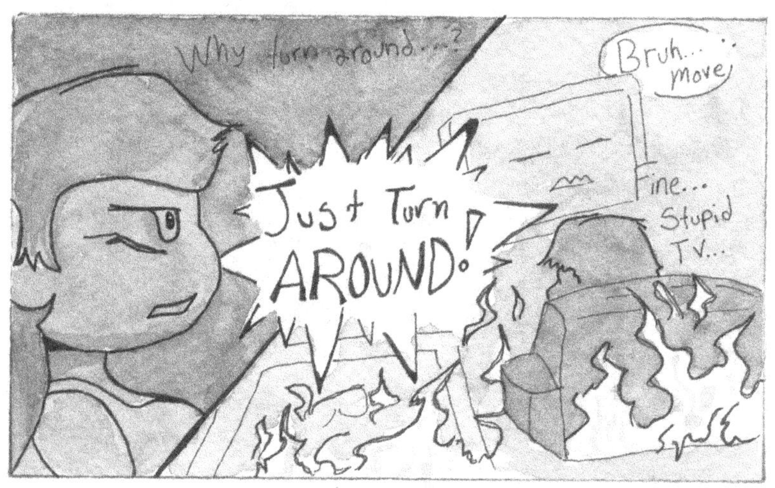

Why turn around...?
Bruh... move
Just Turn AROUND!
Fine... Stupid Tv...

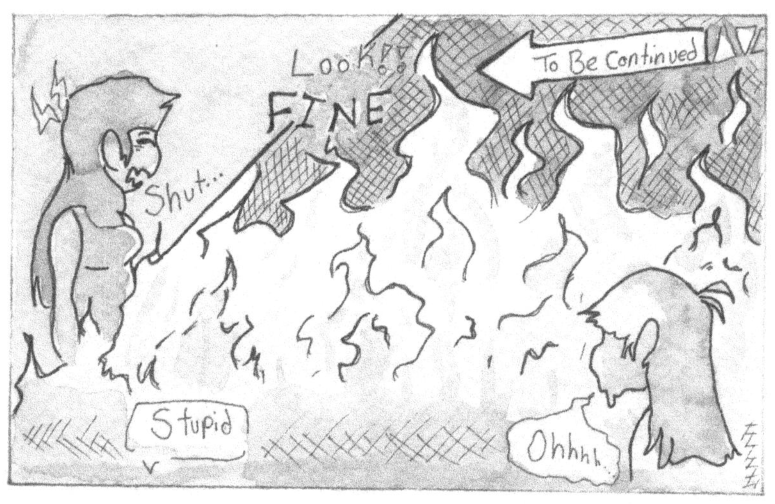

Look!!!
FINE
To Be Continued
Shut...
Stupid
Ohhhh

Panels 7-9
Illustrator: Alina Jones; Ink: Mason Higgins; Ink Wash: Dempsey Langan

TiNY ICKY DOG

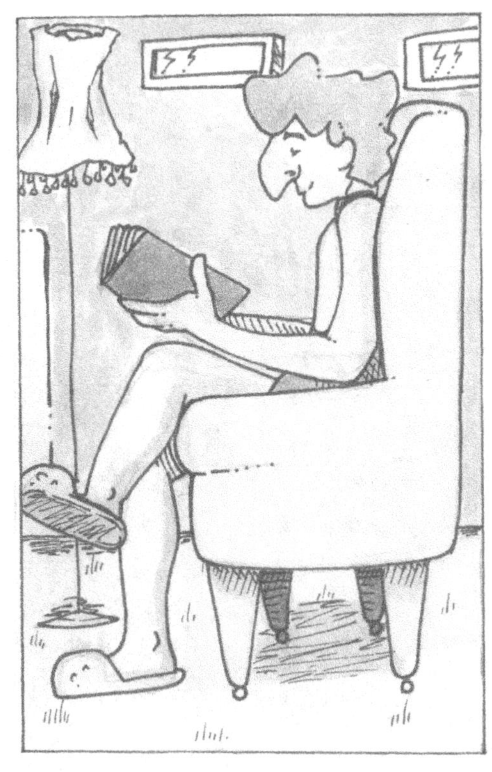

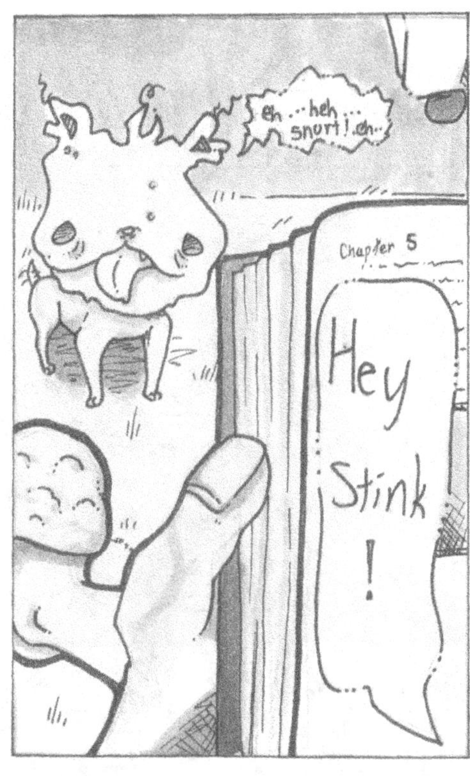

eh...heh...
snort!..eh..
Chapter 5
Hey
Stink
!

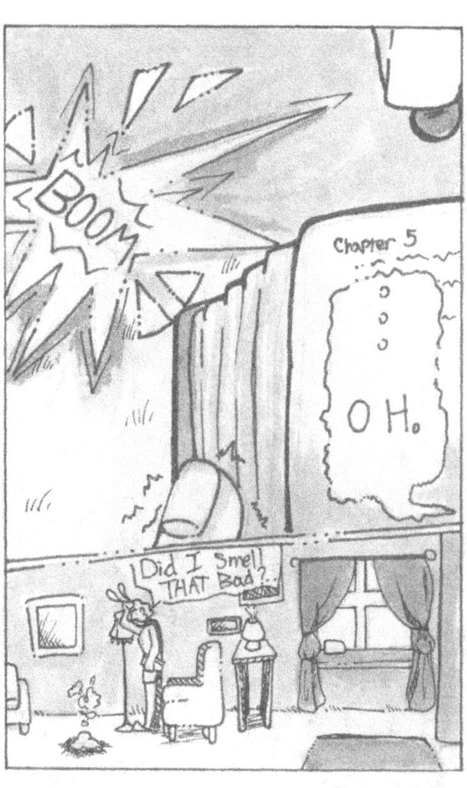

BOOM
Chapter 5
O H.
Did I smell THAT Bad?

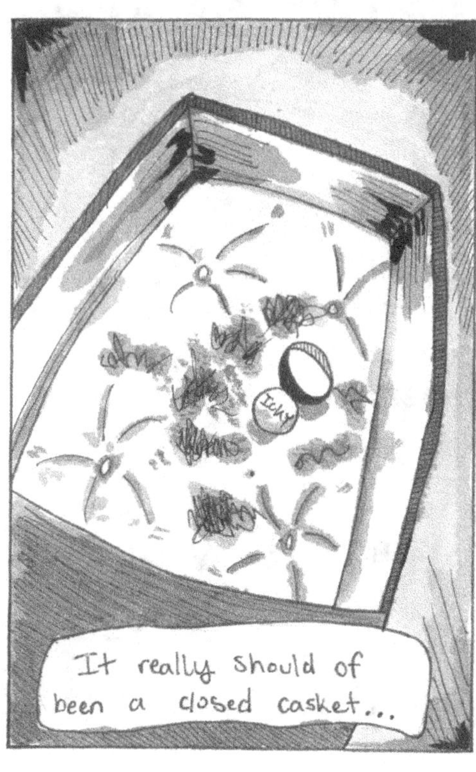

Icky
It really should of been a closed casket...

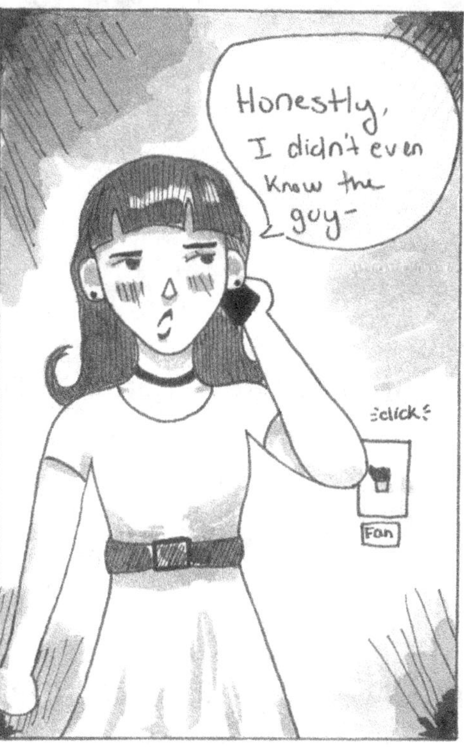

Honestly, I didn't even know the guy-
click
Fan

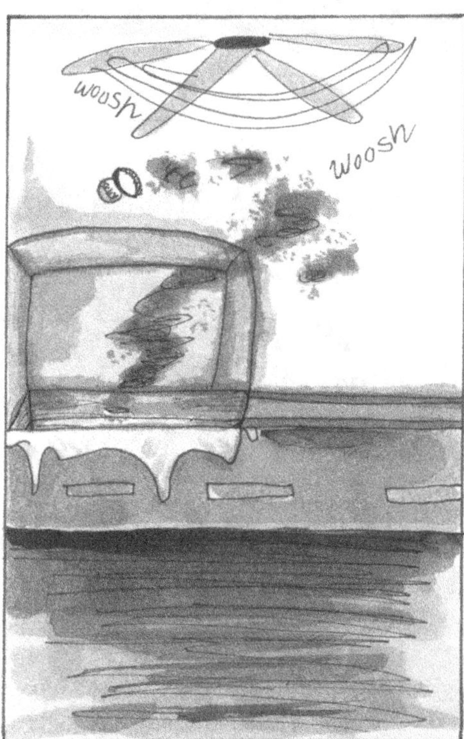

woosh
woosh

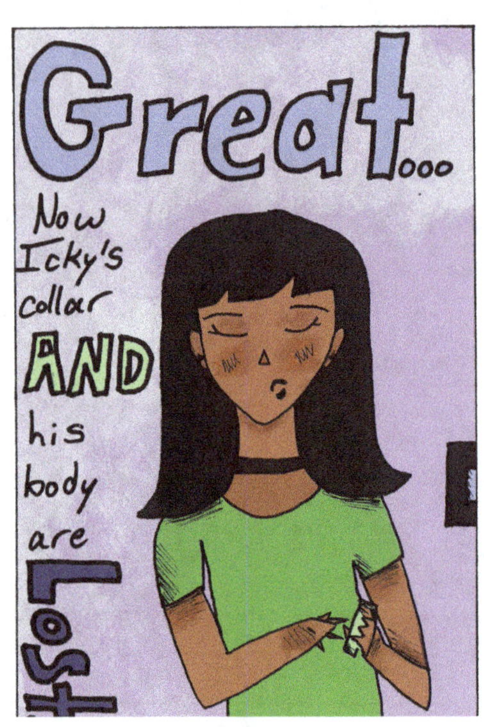
Great...
Now Icky's collar AND his body are Lost

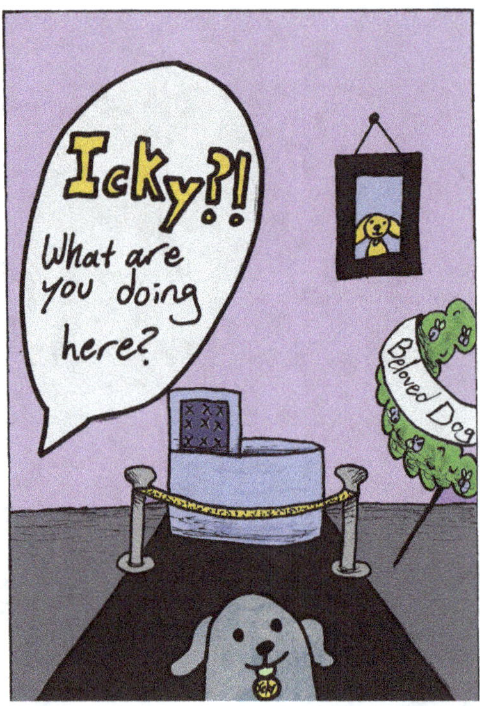
Icky?! What are you doing here?
Beloved Dog

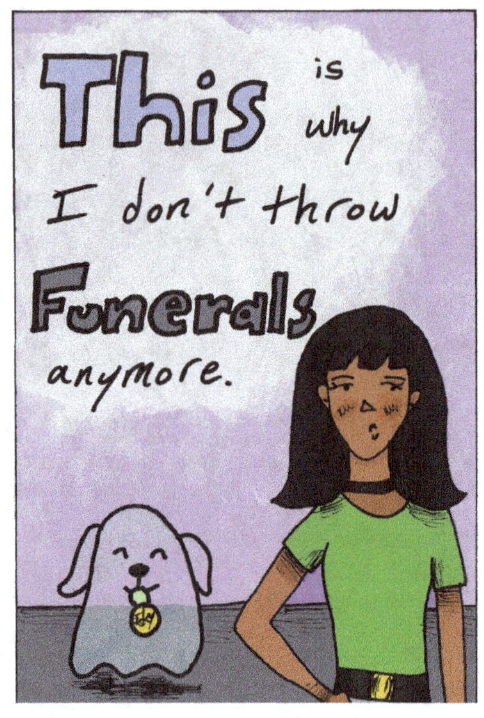
This is why I don't throw Funerals anymore.

TiNY ICKY DOG

Panels 1-3
Illustrator: Kalista Weed; Ink and Ink Wash: Alina Jones;

Panels 4-6
Illustrator: Brianna Vongmany; Ink: Kiersten Kozlowski; Ink Wash: Kalista Weed

Panels 7-9
Illustrator and Ink: Emily Brier; Digital Color: Spike Harris

BABY WAR LEADER

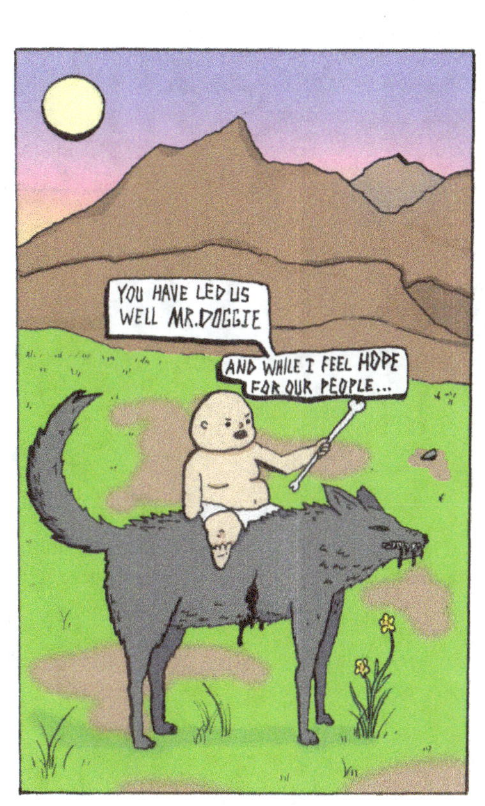

YOU HAVE LED US WELL MR.DOGGIE
AND WHILE I FEEL HOPE FOR OUR PEOPLE...

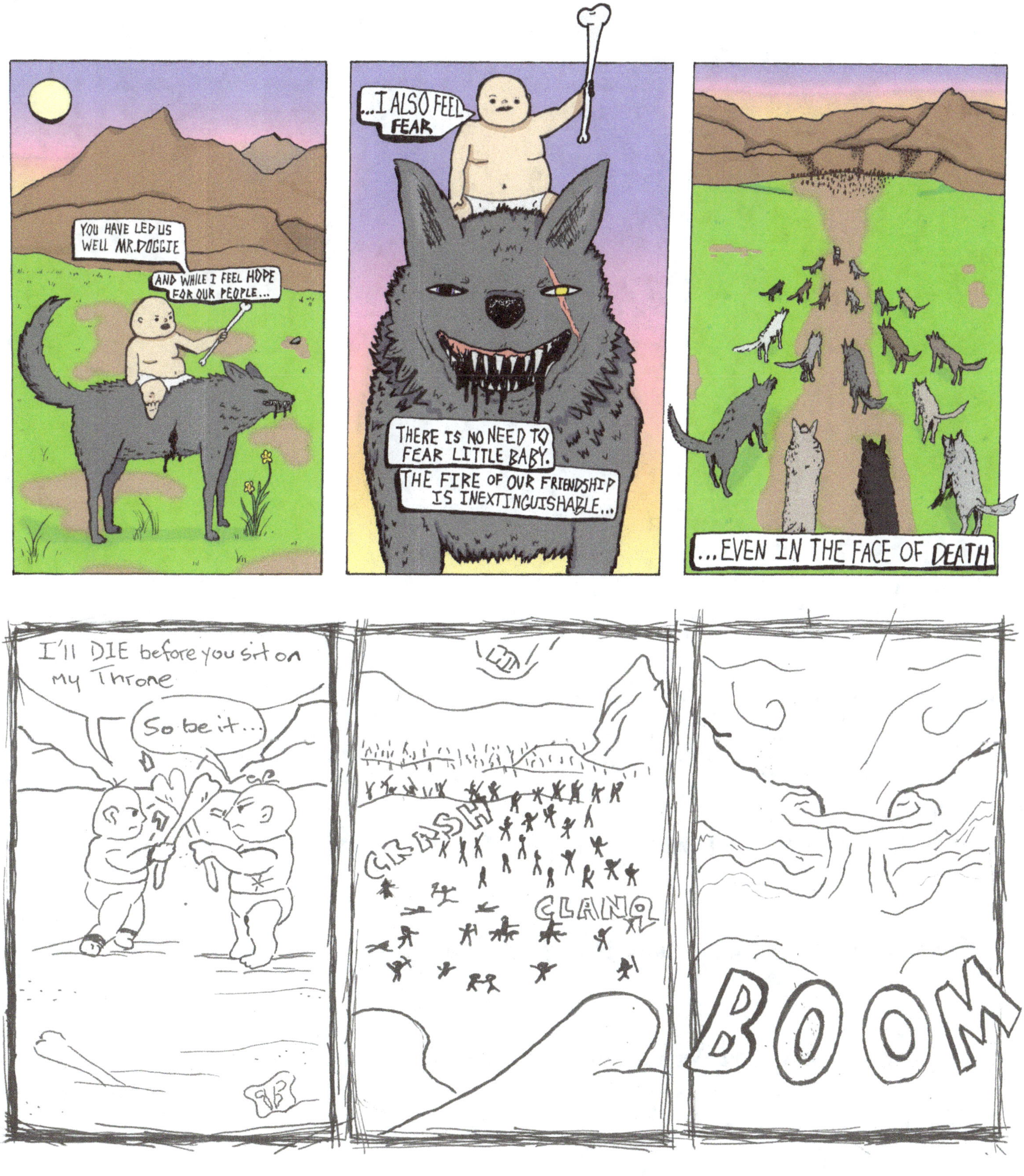

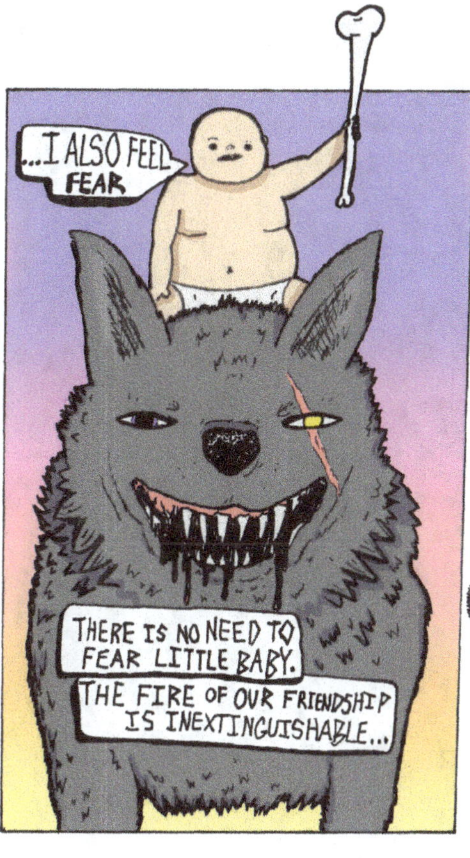

...I ALSO FEEL FEAR
THERE IS NO NEED TO FEAR LITTLE BABY.
THE FIRE OF OUR FRIENDSHIP IS INEXTINGUISHABLE...

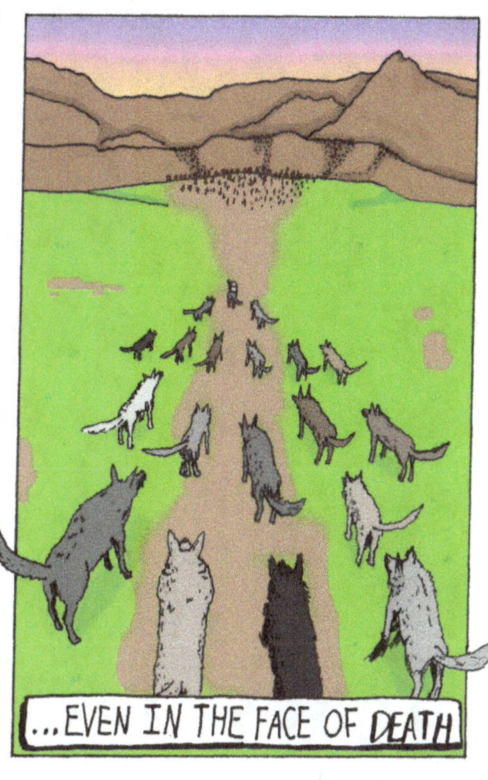

...EVEN IN THE FACE OF DEATH

I'll DIE before you sit on my Throne
So be it...
CRASH
CLANQ
BOOM

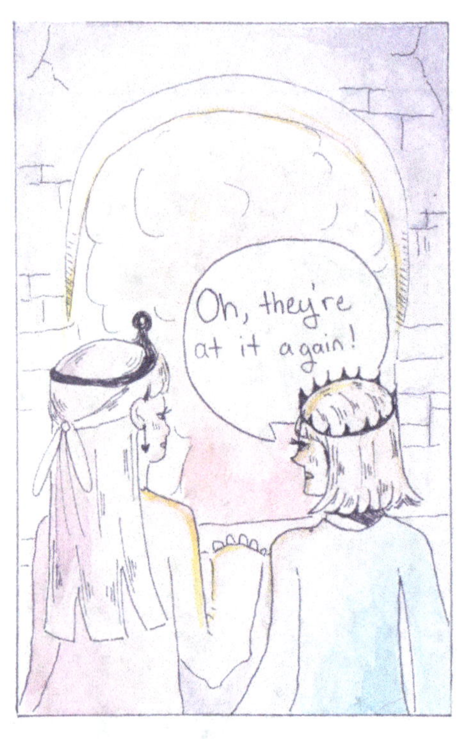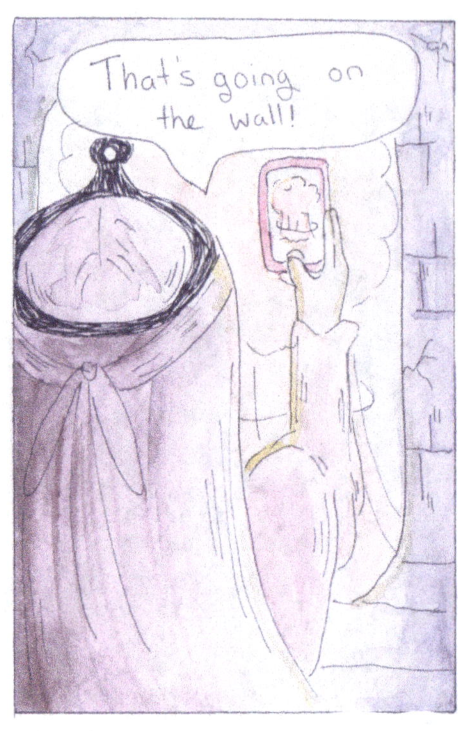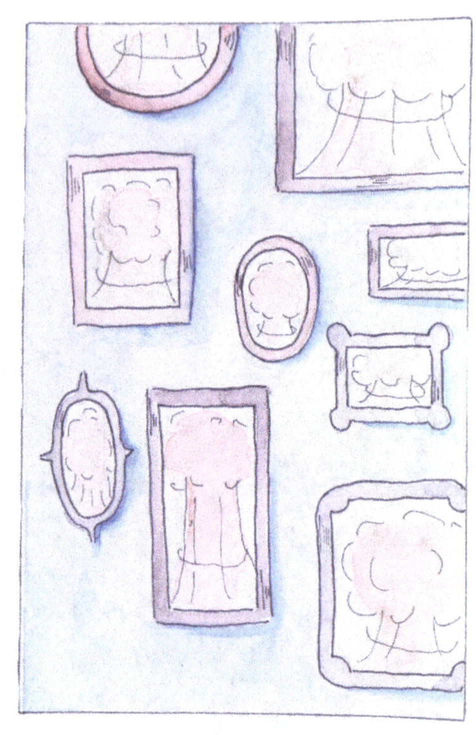

Oh, they're at it again!
That's going on the wall!

BABY WAR LEADER

Panels 1-3
Illustrator and Ink: Dempsey Langan; Digital Color: Nicole Kolakowski

Panels 4-6
Illustrator: Ryan Ackerman; Ink: Theodore Fuller

Panels 7-9
Illustrator, Ink, and Watercolor: Brianna Vongmany